"YOU HAVE NO RIGHT
TO BE DOING THIS," MARY SAID.

"I'm not doing anything, Mary, except trying to get some answers. Which, I might add, could help your husband. I don't believe he murdered Rory Brent."

"You don't?" Mary said. "What makes you such an expert? You write books, that's all. The evidence is against him, as sad as that might be. Please leave."

"Fair enough."

As I reached for the doorknob, I was startled by the sound of heavy footsteps on the porch outside. My hand froze in mid-motion. There was no need for me to open the door because Jake Walther did. He pushed it open with such force that it almost knocked me over. He stepped inside and slammed the door behind him.

He had a crazed look in his eyes.

The smell of alcohol on his breath was overwhelming.

And the sight of the shotgun he carried was sobering.

A LITTLE YULETIDE MURDER

A *Murder, She Wrote*
Mystery

A Novel by Jessica Fletcher
and Donald Bain
based on the
Universal television series
created by Peter S. Fischer,
Richard Levinson & William Link

A SIGNET BOOK

SIGNET
Published by the Penguin Group
Penguin Putnam USA Inc., 375 Hudson Street,
New York, New York 10014, U.S.A.
Penguin Books Ltd, 27 Wrights Lane,
London W8 5TZ, England
Penguin Books Australia Ltd, Ringwood,
Victoria, Australia
Penguin Books Canada Ltd, 10 Alcorn Avenue,
Toronto, Ontario, Canada M4V 3B2
Penguin Books (N.Z.) Ltd, 182–190 Wairau Road,
Auckland 10, New Zealand

Penguin Books Ltd, Registered Offices:
Harmondsworth, Middlesex, England

First published by Signet, an imprint of Dutton NAL,
a member of Penguin Putnam Inc.

First Printing, October, 1998
10 9 8 7 6

REGISTERED TRADEMARK—MARCA REGISTRADA

Printed in the United States of America

PUBLISHER'S NOTE
This is a work of fiction. Names, characters, places, and incidents either are
the product of the author's imagination or are used fictitiously, and any resem-
blance to actual persons, living or dead, events, or locales is entirely
coincidental.

For Zachary, Alexander, and Jacob,
through whose innocent eyes the mystery,
majesty, and promise of the
Christmas spirit lives.

And for Roy Kramer, lawyer and accountant,
who defines what friendship means,
and Billie Kramer, his partner in decency.

Chapter One

"The meeting will come to order!"

We'd gathered in the Cabot Cove Memorial Hall, built after World War II to honor those from our town who'd given their lives, literally and figuratively, defending the country. It soon became a popular place for meetings and social events, especially when large numbers of people were involved. This meeting to plan the upcoming annual Christmas festival certainly qualified. The hall was packed with citizens, most of whom came simply to listen—or to get out of the house during that dreary first week of December—and for some, to offer their ideas on how this year's festival should be conducted.

Cabot Cove's Christmas festival had started small a couple of dozen years ago, consisting back then of townspeople getting together on Christmas Eve and going from house to house to enjoy cider and cookies, singing carols all the way. But as the years passed, the festival became more ambitious. Today it evolves over an entire week, and has become one of Maine's leading tourist attractions. People come from all over to participate in what's been billed as "America's most traditional Christmas celebration." Hotels, inns, and bed-and-breakfasts for miles around are booked as much as a year ahead. Some claimed it had gotten out of hand, becoming too commercialized. Others reveled in the town's national reputation as an oasis in a commercial Christmas world, where tradition reigns. No matter what the view, the festival had taken on a life of its own, and most Cabot Cove citizens got caught up in the excitement and were enthusiastic participants.

I was delighted to be there, not only because I enjoyed participating in the planning, but because for the first time in a few years I would actually be home during the holiday season. I'd found myself traveling on previous holidays, usually to promote my newest murder mystery, or sometimes simply because invitations extended me were too appealing to pass up. But even though I'd spent previous Christmases in some wonderful, even exotic locations, I always felt a certain ache and emptiness at being away from my dear friends, and from the town I loved and called home.

The meeting was being chaired by our mayor, Jim Shevlin. Seated with him at a long table on a raised platform were representatives from the public library, the Chamber of Commerce, the town historic society (sometimes snidely known as the "town hysterical society"), local political clubs, the fire and police departments, the volunteer ambulance corps, and local hospital, schools, and, of course, the standing decorating committee, which each year turned our lovely small village into a festival of holiday lights.

Shevlin again called for order. People eventually took seats and ended their conversations.

"It's gratifying to see so many of you here this morning," Shevlin said, an engaging smile breaking across his handsome Irish face. "This promises to be the biggest and best holiday festival ever."

People applauded, including me and Dr. Seth Hazlitt, my good friend with whom I sat in the front row. He leaned close to my ear and said, "Jimmy always says it's going to be the biggest and the best."

I raised my eyebrows, looked at him, and said, "And it usually is."

"Hard for you to say, Jessica, considerin' you haven't been here in a spell to make comparisons."

"But from what I hear, each year tops the previous one. Besides, I'll be here *this* year."

"And a good thing you will," Seth said. "This is where Jessica Fletcher ought to be spendin' her Christmases."

I was used to mild admonishment from Seth,

knowing he always meant well, even though his tone could be taken at times as being harsh and scolding. I returned my attention to the dais, where Shevlin introduced the chairwoman of the decorating committee. She went through a long list of things the committee planned to do this year, including renting for the first time a large searchlight to project red and green lights into the sky above the town. This resulted in a heated debate about whether a searchlight was too commercial and tacky for Cabot Cove. Eventually, Mayor Shevlin suggested the searchlight idea be put on hold until further discussions could be held.

As such meetings tend to do, this one dragged on beyond a reasonable length. It seemed everyone wanted to have a say, and did. During the presentation of how the schoolchildren would participate I noticed someone missing at the dais. I turned to Seth. "Where's Rory?" I asked.

Seth leaned forward and scanned faces at the long head table. "You're right, Jessica," he said. "Rory hasn't missed a holiday planning meeting for as long as I can remember."

Rory Brent was a prosperous local farmer who'd played Santa Claus at our holiday festival for the past fifteen years. He was born to the role. Brent was a big, outgoing man with a ready, infectious laugh. He easily weighed two hundred and fifty pounds, and had a full head of flowing white hair and a bushy white beard to match. No makeup needed. He *was* Santa Claus. His custom was to attend the planning meeting fully dressed in his Santa costume, which he proudly dragged out of mothballs each year, stitched up gaps in the seams, had cleaned and pressed, and wore to the meeting.

"Is he ill?" I asked.

"Saw him yesterday," Seth said. "Down to Charlene's Bakery. Looked healthy enough to me."

"He must have been detained. Maybe some emergency at the farm."

"Ayuh," Seth muttered.

A few minutes later, when Jim Shevlin invited further comments from the audience, Seth stood and asked why Rory Brent wasn't there.

"I had Margaret try to call him at the farm," Shevlin said. Margaret was deputy mayor of Cabot Cove. He looked to where she sat to his right.

She reported into her microphone, "I called a few times but there's no answer."

"Maybe somebody ought to take a ride out to the farm," Seth suggested from the floor.

"Good idea," said Shevlin. "Any volunteers?"

Tim Purdy, a member of the Chamber of Commerce, whose business was managing farms around the United States from his office in Cabot Cove, said he'd check on Rory, and left the hall.

"You can always count on Tim," said Seth, sitting.

The meeting lasted another half hour. Although

there was disagreement on a number of issues, it warmed my heart to see how the citizens of the town could come together and negotiate their differences.

Coffee, tea, juice, and donuts were served at the rear of the hall, and I enjoyed apple juice and a cinnamon donut with friends, many of whom expressed pleasure that I would be in town for the festivities.

"I was wondering whether you would do a Christmas reading for the kids this year, Jessica," Cynthia Curtis, director of our library and a member of the town board, said.

"I'd love to," I replied. "Some traditional Christmas stories? Fables?"

"Whatever you choose to do," she said.

But then I thought of Seth, who was chatting in a far corner with our sheriff and another good friend, Morton Metzger.

"Seth usually does the reading, doesn't he?" I said.

"Oh, I don't think he'd mind deferring to you this year, Jess. It would be a special treat for the kids to have a famous published author read Christmas stories to them."

I suppose my face expressed concern about usurping Seth.

"Why don't you do the reading together?" Cynthia suggested. "That would be a different approach."

I liked that idea, and said so. "I'll discuss it with Seth as soon as we leave."

Seth and Mort approached.

"Feel like an early lunch?" Seth asked.

"Sure. Nice presentation, Mort," I said, referring to the report he'd given about how the police department would maintain order during the festival.

"Been doing it long enough," he said. "Ought to know what's needed. 'Course, never have to worry about anybody gettin' too much out of hand. Folks really pick up on the Christmas spirit around here, love thy neighbor, that sort of thing."

We decided to have lunch at Mara's Luncheonette, down by the water and a favorite local hangout. The weather was cold and nasty; snow was forecast.

"I hope Mara made up some of her clam chowder," I said as the three of us prepared to leave. "Chowder and fresh baked bread is appealing."

We reached the door and were in the process of putting on our coats when Tim Purdy entered. I knew immediately from his expression that something was wrong. He came directly to Sheriff Metzger and said something to him we couldn't hear. Mort's face turned serious, too.

"What's wrong?" I asked.

"There's been an accident out at Rory's place," Purdy said.

"An accident? To Rory?" Seth asked.

"Afraid so," said Purdy. "Rory is dead!"

"Rory is dead?" Seth and I said in unison.

Purdy nodded, grimly.

"Means Santa's dead, too," Seth said.

He was right. My eyes filled as I said, "I'm suddenly not hungry."

Chapter Two

Although the sad news of Rory Brent's death had taken away any appetite I might have had minutes earlier, I succumbed to Seth's insistence that I go with him to Mara's, if only to keep him company. Sheriff Metzger had immediately left for Brent's farm to investigate the situation.

By the time we got to Mara's—only ten minutes or so after learning the news from Tim Purdy—the report of Brent's death had reached every corner of Cabot Cove.

"What terrible news," Mara said as we entered her small, popular waterfront eatery. "Can't hardly believe it."

"We're all in shock," I replied as she led Seth and me to a window table.

"Any word on how he died?" Mara asked.

"Not so far as I know," said Seth, adding, "Rory was a big man, carried too much weight. Hauling around that kind of tonnage puts a strain on the heart. I told him every time he came in for a checkup to drop a few pounds, but he'd just laugh and say he liked having more of him for folks to love."

I couldn't help but smile at that reference to Rory Brent. He was perpetually jovial; people like him warm the hearts of others. He'd be missed, not only because our familiar Santa Claus wouldn't be here this Christmas, but because we wouldn't be the recipients of his sunny disposition the rest of the year.

Seth and I sat in silence after Mara left us to greet new customers. We looked out the window onto the town dock and beyond, where a heavy, wet, cold fog had settled in over the water, obscuring all but the nearest boats. I thought of Rory's wife, Patricia, as shy and reticent a person as her husband was gregarious.

Patricia Brent stayed pretty much to herself on the farm, running the household and addressing every one of her husband's needs. A dutiful wife was the way to describe her, although I was sure she had many other dimensions than that. They had a son, Robert. Thinking of him made me wince.

Robert Brent, who'd just turned eighteen, did not share his father's positive reputation around town. A brooding young man, he'd had more than one run-in with Sheriff Mort Metzger, usually after a night of drinking with his buddies. Although he lived on the farm with his mother and father, people who knew them better than I did said he seldom lifted a finger to help out, preferring instead to sit in his room, reading magazines about guns and hot automobiles and the military. I don't think I'd ever had a conversation with the younger Brent, my direct contact with him consisting only of an occasional greeting from me on the street, which was usually not returned.

He was different from his father in another way, too. Robert Brent was as thin as his father was corpulent. To further set him apart—perhaps a continuation of his teenage rebellious years—he had shaved his head, making the contrast with his father's flowing white hair that much more dramatic. But although I was not particularly fond of Robert Brent, my heart went out to him at that moment, as well as to his mother, Patricia. As traumatic as Rory's death was for the community, it was surely devastating to them.

Seth ordered his usual, a fried clam sandwich and small green salad. Mara had made clam chowder that day, and I ordered a bowl, nothing else.

"I assume it was a heart attack," I said idly, tasting the chowder which was, no surprise, superb.

"Perhaps," Seth said. "Or stroke. I suppose we'll find out soon enough."

"Will there be an autopsy?" I asked.

"I suspect so. Doc Treyz will probably be asked to do one, considerin' the sudden nature of Rory's death. Standard procedure in cases like this."

I looked up at him and said, "I didn't realize that. I thought it was standard procedure only when the cause of death was suspicious."

"Ayuh," Seth said, taking another bite of his sandwich, which he'd slathered with Mara's homemade tartar sauce. "We'll just have to see what Mort comes up with, whether he labels it suspicious. Eat your chowder, Jessica, 'fore it gets cold as outdoors."

We fell silent for a few more minutes until I said, "Not a very cheery Christmas for Patricia Brent."

"I wouldn't argue that with you," Seth said, sitting back and wiping tartar sauce from the corner of his mouth with a napkin. "Never easy losing someone any time of year, but especially tough around Christmas."

"I wonder who'll be chosen to be Santa this year," I said.

"Up to the committee," Seth said.

"Cynthia Curtis suggested that you and I read Christmas stories to the kids together this year."

His eyes went up. "Did she now?"

"Of course, I wouldn't think of joining you unless you really wanted me to."

"Seems like a right good idea, Jessica. I like it."

I drew a deep breath and also sat back in my

chair. Funny, I thought, how quickly we return to mundane, everyday matters so soon after someone dies. Here we were discussing the Christmas festivities as though nothing had happened to Rory.

Seth evidently sensed what I was thinking because he said, "Life goes on, Jessica. That's the way it was meant to be by the good Lord up above. Festival is real important to Cabot Cove. Rory would have wanted us to get on with it, make it the biggest and best ever. Coffee?"

Mara had made pecan pie that morning. I passed it up, but Seth enjoyed a hearty serving. We finished our coffee and had stood to leave when Mort Metzger came through the doorway. He was immediately asked by others about what information he had concerning Rory Brent's death, but he ignored them and came to us.

"Cup 'a coffee, Mort?" Seth asked.

"Don't mind if I do," our sheriff said, removing his Stetson hat and sitting heavily in a third chair at the table.

Mara came to take our new order, but lingered at the table after we'd told her we wanted three coffees. Mort ignored her presence and said, "Looks like we've got ourselves a little Yuletide murder on our hands."

Seth and I looked at each other, eyes narrowed, brows furrowed.

"Rory Brent has been murdered?" Mara said loudly.

Mort nodded, looked up at her, and said, "Seems that way, Mara. Got any pecan pie left?"

She left the table. Seth and I leaned closer to Mort. Seth said, "Now, Morton, be a little more specific. Are you certain it was murder?"

"Certainly looks that way to me, Doc. Gunshot to the left temple. Didn't exit the other side, so the bullet is still in his brain. Must have dropped instantly."

I said, "Why are you so sure it was murder? Couldn't it have been suicide?"

"Surely not, Mrs. F. No weapon at the scene. Of course, I'm saying he was shot based upon my examination of him. Could be something else was involved along with a gun. Doc Treyz will have to come to that determination. The ambulance boys were out there real fast, took poor old Rory away."

"Where was the body?" I asked.

"Out in one of his barns. The big one at the back of the property." A puzzled expression crossed Mort's face. "Funny," he said, mostly to himself.

"What's funny?" Seth asked.

"Rory was out there in shirtsleeves. No coat, no hat, no gloves. Can't imagine him trekkin' all the way from the house out to the barn in this weather without winter clothing."

"Maybe he just ran out there to get something quick," I offered.

"That barn has got to be a half mile from the

house. You don't run out there to get something quick," Mort said.

I didn't argue with him.

"How's Patricia?" Seth asked.

"She wasn't there," Mort said.

"That's unusual, isn't it?" I said. "She seems always to be at the farm."

"I wouldn't know about that," said Mort, sticking his fork into the pie Mara had set in front of him. "His crazy kid was there, though."

"Was he the one who discovered the body?" I asked.

"According to Tim Purdy. Tim said he got out there just a few minutes after Robert found Rory in the barn. Robert said he was about to call my office when Tim arrived. Says he figured since Tim was coming back to town to tell us, there was no need for him to make a call."

"I assume he was upset," I said.

"You can't prove it by me, Mrs. F. That kid is a real foul ball. Just had that dumb, placid expression on his skinny little face. Didn't hardly say nothing."

"What was he doing when you arrived?" Seth asked.

"Sittin' in his room, reading magazines."

"After just discovering that his father had been killed?" I said, unable to keep the incredulity from my voice.

"Like I said, he's a strange-o. The only thing he said was about Jake Walther."

"What about Jake?" Seth asked.

"He said I should go arrest the old son-of-a— no need to repeat his profanity," Mort said, looking at me. "He said I should arrest Jake for killing his father."

"Does he know that for a fact?" I asked.

Mort shook his head and ate more pie.

"Everybody knows Rory and Jake Walther had bad blood between them," Seth said.

"But that doesn't matter," I said. "What would cause Robert Brent to immediately accuse Jake of having killed his father?"

"Beats me," Mort said. "I told the boy I'd be back to question him."

"Did he mention his mother?" I asked.

"Says she went to visit somebody. A cousin. Well, I'd better get back there and get answers to some questions I didn't get around to asking. I suppose seeing good ol' Rory lyin' dead in his barn shook me up a little. Not supposed to, being an officer of the law and all that. But I'm human."

"Mind if I come along?" I asked.

"I suppose not, Mrs. F., although there's not much to see. My boys took pictures of the scene and did all their measuring before the ambulance took Rory away. Just a crude sketch on the dirt floor where he was found."

"I'd like to go," I said. "Maybe Patricia Brent is

there and could use some comforting. You know, woman-to-woman."

"Sounds like a good idea," Seth said. "I'd come with you, too, except I've got a full slate of patients this afternoon, starting—" He looked at his watch. "Starting ten minutes ago. Excuse me. Call you later at home, Jessica."

Chapter Three

The landscape of Cabot Cove has changed quite a bit over the years I've called it home. It still retains a small-town charm, but is no longer the sleepy little coastal Maine village it once was.

The change isn't especially apparent downtown because most of the shops continue to be owned by individuals, rather than chains and large corporations. The best coffee shop is not a Starbucks, and the largest clothing store is called Charles, not the Gap or Eddie Bauer or Jos. Bank.

But as you leave the center of town and proceed north on an extension of Main Street, the effects of "progress" become readily apparent. All the major fast-food companies have an outlet along that stretch of road, and there are now two strip-malls housing a couple of major department stores and trendy boutiques. However, unlike many towns and villages across America, the opening of the malls did not put local downtown merchants out of business. Cabot Coveites are a resilient lot, one of many things I love about living here.

I sat in the front seat of Mort's sheriff's car and watched the sights go by as we continued north until the malls, hamburger places, and gas stations faded from view and we were in tranquil farm country. The area doesn't support the farming industry as it once did, but there are still plenty of hearty souls who, having had their farms handed down from generation to generation, continue to work the soil and take from it both enough money to live, and a psychic pleasure only farmers understand.

As we approached Rory Brent's spread, Mort said, "I just keep thinking of poor ol' Rory no longer being alive. I really liked that man. I suppose everybody in town did."

"That's a fair assessment, Mort. Not only was he likable, I was always impressed at his skill at farming. It's not an easy way to make a living, but he certainly seemed to have the knack."

"No thanks to that worthless kid of his," Mort grumbled, turning into the long, tree-lined road leading up to the Brent house, which sat majestically on a rise, affording views in every direction of the hundreds of acres surrounding it.

Not that there was much to see that day. The clouds had lowered, obscuring the horizon.

We pulled up in front of the house and got out. The Brent residence looked the way a farmhouse should look. An inviting covered porch spanned the front. The main part of the house was painted a pale yellow, the shutters and front door a forest green. It was more than a hundred years old, but had been meticulously maintained. The paint was fresh, the grounds manicured. The only artifact giving away its twentieth-century occupants was a huge satellite dish off to one side.

We stepped up onto the porch, and Mort knocked. When no one responded, he knocked again, louder this time. A chill went through me as I stood there, and I pulled my coat a little closer about me. Eventually, the door opened, and we faced Rory and Patricia's son, Robert.

"I said I'd be back," Mort said. "Did your mom return yet?"

"No," he replied flatly, the morose, sullen expression never changing on his thin, sallow face.

"You haven't heard from her?"

"No."

"Well, Mrs. Fletcher and I are going back out to the barn. You aren't planning to go anywhere, are you, Bob?"

"No."

With that, he closed the door, leaving us standing on the porch. Mort mumbled something under his breath—I assumed it was just as well that I didn't hear what he said—and we came down off the porch, went around the side of the house, and headed for the barn that was partially veiled by the low clouds. Two vehicles were parked in front of it, one a marked police car, the other a vehicle without markings.

"The boys are still going over the scene," Mort said as we trudged along a narrow path. We'd almost reached the barn when one of Mort's deputies stepped outside.

"Just wrappin' things up here," the deputy said.

"Who belongs to that other car?" Mort asked.

"County police," the young deputy replied. His name was Tom Coleman; he'd been a Cabot Cove police officer for less than a year.

"How'd they get involved so fast?" Mort asked, leading the way into the barn.

"Didn't ask 'em," Coleman said, closing the door behind us. Not that it mattered whether the door was open or closed. It was as cold in the barn as it had been outside.

Two men in suits stood by the crude outline of where Rory's body had been. Mort introduced himself, and they did the same.

"I wish you hadn't had the body moved so quickly," one of them said.

"Didn't see any need to leave him lyin' on the ground," Mort said. His attempt to keep annoyance out of his voice was unsuccessful. "I *horsed* him right out of here."

The two county officers looked at each other. One asked, "Did you personally examine the body before it was removed?"

"Of course I did," Mort said. "Took a real close look at it. Checked the area for any physical evidence, weapons, notes, things like that. Nothing there. Checked for footprints. Didn't see any that wouldn't have been made by the deceased."

"Was the door to the barn open?" one of the men asked.

"*Ayuh.* I wasn't the one who discovered the body."

"You weren't?"

"No. The son did. A fella named Tim Purdy came back into town and reported that Mr. Brent was dead. That's when I came out here. Didn't know whether it had been an accident or what. When I got here, I took a close look at Rory's head. Single bullet hole to the left temple. No exit wound. No weapon. Checked for rigor. Body was getting cold, but still had a little heat left. Rigor was just setting in. I pegged time of death between two and four hours earlier."

Mort had obviously done the right thing when investigating the scene, and I was proud of him. There are people who sometimes view the Cabot Cove police department as being run by country bumpkins, but that certainly isn't true. Although Mort occasionally comes off as being unsure of himself, he'd kept pace with scientific advancement in police work ever since he became our sheriff years ago, and has a mind that is a lot keener than is sometimes apparent at first meeting.

The men had been talking to Mort as though I didn't exist. Suddenly, they seemed to discover I was there and looked at me.

"This is Jessica Fletcher," Mort said.

"The famous mystery writer," one of the county officers said, extending his hand.

"I don't know about famous, but I do write murder mysteries," I said.

"Any special reason you're here?" the other officer in civilian clothes asked.

"No. Mort told me what had happened out here, and I came along. Rory Brent was a friend of mine, a much loved individual in Cabot Cove."

"I just thought you might be out here getting material for your next mystery novel," the officer said, smiling.

"Never entered my mind," I said.

They turned their attention again to Mort. "Interview any suspects?" he was asked.

"Talked to the son, Robert. He's up in the house. The wife, Patricia, went downstate to visit a cousin, according to the son. Says she was due back a couple of hours ago."

One of the men said to the other, "Let's go up and talk to the kid."

"Now hold on a second," Mort said. "This murder occurred in my jurisdiction, and I'm responsible for the investigation. Perfectly fine for you county fellas to get involved with the autopsy, that sort of thing. But when it comes to questioning people, I'll take care of that."

Mort and the men looked at each other without another word being spoken. Finally, one of them said to the other, "Let's go," then turned to Mort. "We'll be back."

"I'll be looking forward to seeing you again," Mort said.

As we prepared to leave the barn to return to the house, Mort instructed his deputy to remain there until relieved. The front of the barn had been cordoned off with yellow crime-scene tape. "Nobody comes in here unless he's official. Got that, Tom?"

"Yes, sir."

"Come on, Mrs. F., let's go have a chat with Mr. Robert Brent."

When we were outside, I asked, "Are you sure you want me with you when you question him?"

"I wouldn't if I was about to *question* him. But I just intend for him and me to have a little chat. Nothing wrong with you being there while we chat, is there?"

"I suppose not."

A few soft snowflakes had begun to fall from the leaden sky. We'd just rounded the corner of the house when Dimitri Cassis pulled up in his taxi. Dimitri is a Greek immigrant who'd settled with his family in Cabot Cove after buying the local taxi service from Jake Monroe, who'd retired. He is a handsome, hardworking man who'd been readily accepted into the community. Because I don't drive, I use his service often, to the extent that I have a house account I pay monthly.

He jumped out of the taxi and opened the rear door, through which Patricia Brent exited, carrying a small tapestry overnight bag.

"She doesn't know," I said quietly to Mort. "My God, what a shock this will be."

Patricia was as small a person as her deceased husband had been big. She was birdlike and wore old-fashioned long, flowered dresses. She kept her graying hair up in a tight bun. When she spotted us approaching, a puzzled frown crossed her face.

"Hello, Patricia," I said. "Jessica Fletcher."

" 'Afternoon, Mrs. Brent," Mort said, tipping his Stetson.

"My goodness," Patricia said, suddenly smiling. "What are you doing here?"

"Afraid we have some bad news," said Mort.

"Bad news?" She said to Dimitri, "I'm sorry. I forgot to pay you."

We watched as she fished money from her purse and handed it to him. He appeared to not want to leave, now that he had heard there was some bad news being reported. But he also instinctively understood that as long as he was present, that bad news was probably not going to be voiced. He thanked her, said hello to Mort and me, got back in his taxi, and drove away.

Patricia took a deep breath, pulled herself up to her maximum height, which was not more than five feet, and said, "Well, now, what is this bad news you have?"

"Maybe we'd better go inside," Mort said. "Starting to snow. Catch a chill out here."

"Of course," she said. "I'll put on a pot of tea— unless you'd like something stronger. We always keep a few bottles in the house, although neither Rory nor I drink."

Mort and I thought the same thing, that their son certainly didn't fall into his parents' teetotaling habits.

We followed her into the house and stood in a large foyer. She placed her bag on the floor, removed her coat, and looked in the mirror, touching hair that had been blown during the taxi ride. "Please, take off your coats," she said.

"Ma'am, I don't think we will be having any tea," Mort said. He looked at me; I gave him a look that said we should take off our coats and go to a more comfortable setting to break the news. He picked up on my silent message, removed his jacket, helped me off with my coat, and we went with Patricia to the living room, a large, pleasant space, dominated by a huge hooked rug, antique pine furniture, and hundreds of knick-knacks.

"Please, sit," she said. "Tea will only take a minute."

"Mrs. Brent, I—"

Mort's words were lost in the room as Patricia suddenly disappeared in the direction of the kitchen.

When she was gone, Mort turned to me and said, "Something strange going on here, Mrs. F."

I nodded.

"Here poor ol' Rory is shot dead not more than six or seven hours ago. I say we got bad news, and she just sits us down in the parlor and goes in to make tea. The son knows what happened, but he doesn't even bother coming down to be with his mother when she finds out."

"I suppose people handle these things in different ways," I said, not really meaning it, but groping for something to say in defense of the Brent family.

"I'm glad you're here," Mort said. "Hate to be breaking the news to her alone."

Patricia returned from the kitchen, now wearing an apron.

"Only take a minute for the water to boil," she said, sitting primly in a straight-back chair across from where we sat side by side on the couch. "Now, what is this bad news you have to give me? It has to do with Rory, doesn't it?"

An uncomfortable glance passed between Mort and me before I said, "Patricia, Rory is dead."

She lowered her head and looked at hands clasped in her lap. She remained in that position for what seemed a very long time, and neither Mort nor I said anything to intrude. Finally, she looked up and said, "What happened? Did he have a heart attack?"

Mort cleared his throat before saying, "Not exactly, ma'am. You see, Rory died out in the barn. He was . . . well, no sense beating around the bush. He was shot dead."

A tiny involuntary gasp came from Patricia Brent. Her eyes went into motion, looking, it seemed, for some answer in corners of the room.

"You say Rory was shot," she said. "Did he kill himself?"

The directness of the question took us both aback. Mort answered, "No, ma'am, it looks to me as though someone killed your husband."

"Oh, my God," she said so softly we barely heard her. "Who would want to do something like that to Rory?"

"That's what I intend to find out," Mort said, injecting official tone into his voice.

"Does Robert know?" she asked.

"Yes, he does," Mort replied. "He's upstairs. At least, he was."

"Poor boy," she said. "Terrible to lose your father that way."

I was becoming increasingly uncomfortable at

her demeanor. She was without affect, her voice a monotone, her eyes seldom blinking.

"Mrs. Brent, Robert told us you were downstate visiting a relative," Mort said.

"Yes. My cousin Jane."

"Down there overnight?" Mort asked.

"No. I took the bus first thing this morning. Jane fell and hurt her ankle. In a big cast. I went down to help out a little bit, but really wasn't needed."

"Where does your cousin live?" Mort asked.

"Salem."

"Salem's only about forty-five minutes from here," Mort said.

"That's right," Patricia said. "Forty minutes exactly on the bus. I timed it."

What time did the bus leave?"

"Seven."

"So you got down there close to eight," Mort said. "What bus did you catch back?"

"The one o'clock. Took longer to come back. An accident tied things up in every direction. Dimitri was at the bus station and drove me home."

"So I saw," Mort said.

"Any idea who might have done this to Rory?" I asked.

She slowly shook her head.

Mort followed with, "Robert told me I should check into Jake Walther."

"Jake? Do you think he killed Rory?"

"I don't know, Patricia, but that's what Bob said."

Patricia thought for a moment before saying, "Rory and Jake never did get along. But then again, I don't know of anyone in the area who gets along with Jake."

"Yes, he is a disagreeable sort," I offered. "Did Rory and Jake have a feud going, some sort of conflict that perhaps became more intense lately?"

"I wouldn't know about that," she said.

She was interrupted by the shrill sound of the teakettle's whistle. "Excuse me," she said, going to the kitchen.

Mort said to me, "I think it's time I had a talk with the son, don't you, Mrs. F.?"

"I suppose so," I said. "But frankly, I'd just as soon not be with you during *that* conversation. Any chance of running me back into town before you question him . . . have your chat?"

"I suppose so, although I want to make sure he doesn't leave here. Come to think of it, maybe he'd be willin' to come with me down to headquarters. Question him in a little more formal surroundings. Might get more done."

"Can you do that without charging him?"

"*Ayuh,* provided he comes willingly. I'm not accusing him of anything, just looking for information. If he wants a lawyer, he can have one."

"Whatever you say, Mort," I said as Patricia returned, carrying a tray with tea, milk, and sugar, and a small plate of cookies.

Mort stood. I did, too. "Patricia, I don't mean to be rude," Mort said, "but Mrs. Fletcher and I have to get back to town. Won't have time for your tea. I thought I might ask Robert to come with us. I have to start getting some information to help in the investigation, and he might be able to offer something."

"Take him to police headquarters?" she asked.

"No, ma'am, not *taking* him there. Just asking him if he'd be willing. I'll be wanting to return and talk to you again, too. My deputy, Tom Coleman, is back in the barn, and he'll be staying until he's relieved. I'd appreciate it if you didn't go anywhere until I have a chance to come back."

"I won't be going anywhere except—"

"Except what?" I asked.

"Except to make funeral arrangements, I suppose. I'll have to do that, won't I?"

"Eventually," Mort answered. "But Doc Treyz will be doing an autopsy on Rory. That's the law."

"Of course. Thank you for coming," she said. "I have a few phone calls to make. Family to be told. You understand?"

"Of course we do," I said. I crossed to where she stood and put my arms around her frail body. She was as rigid as an oak, and I quickly backed away.

"Would you be good enough to ask Robert to come down?" Mort said.

"Yes. I'll go up to his room right now. He spends a lot of time there, you know, reading. He likes to read. He's very intelligent."

Chapter Four

Judging from Robert Brent's loud, angry voice, which was clearly heard in the living room, he wasn't keen on coming downstairs. But Patricia prevailed. Five minutes later, he followed her into the living room. He wore jeans, ankle-high military-style boots, a blue sweatshirt with gold figures on it that looked like some sort of military ranger group's, and a blue baseball cap worn backward.

"Robert, you know Sheriff Metzger and Mrs. Fletcher," Patricia said.

His response was to glare at us.

Mort said, "Thought you wouldn't mind coming down with me to town, Robert. You know, just to have a little chat about what happened to your dad."

Robert looked at his mother, who smiled demurely and nodded.

"Won't take very long," Mort added. "Of course, if you'd rather not, we can talk here."

"About Jake Walther?" Robert asked.

Mort looked at me before saying, "Sure. We can talk about Jake. Talk about anything you'd like."

"I'm not being arrested or anything, am I?" Robert asked. "I didn't do anything. Jake shot my father."

Mort's chuckle was forced. "Of course you're not being arrested for anything, Bob. Like I said, you could help me understand a little bit more about what happened. I'd be right interested in hearing about Jake Walther and why you think he might have shot your father."

"Not *might* have shot my father," Robert said angrily. "He did it."

"You saw him do it?" I asked, surprised at how adamant he was.

Robert ignored my question and said to Mort, "I don't mind going with you. Are we driving in your car?"

Mort nodded. "Unless you'd rather come in your own."

Robert shook his head. "I'll come with you." He looked at me. "Are you coming, too?"

"Yes," I said. "Sheriff Metzger drove me out here and will bring me home. But I won't be with you when you and the sheriff have your talk."

That seemed to satisfy him.

While the conversation was taking place, I observed Patricia Brent. Living in a semirural part of the country had put me in contact with many farmers, men and women who live off the soil and were not unduly touched by the world's modern thinking. They tend to be a stoic lot. I don't mean that in a disparaging way. It's just that it has been my experience that such people are not glib, much to their credit. There is too much glibness in the world as far as I'm concerned.

But at a time like this, when a loved one has been found murdered, you would expect even the most dour of individuals to display some emotion, some sign of deep pain and hurt. Not so with Patricia. She was as calm and placid as though we were there picking up her son to take him to a basketball game. I had to remind myself to not be judgmental. Each of us handles grief in his or her own way. When my husband, Frank, died years ago, I fought to retain my composure and to deal with the death of this man I loved very much in a rational and controlled manner. Did people look at me the way I was looking at Patricia at this moment, wondering why I was not displaying the emotion *they* expected of me? Of course, there were countless moments alone when I broke down and allowed my grief to pour out in a torrent of tears. Perhaps that's what would happen the moment we left. Patricia Brent would go to her room, close the door, and cry her heart out.

"Ready?" Mort asked Robert.

"I have to get my coat," he said.

"Good idea," Mort said. "Nasty day out there, and gettin' worse."

Robert returned from the vestibule, wearing a black-and-red wool mackinaw.

"You take care, Mrs. Brent," Mort said, touching Patricia on the shoulder. "Just give yell if there's anything I can do for you."

"And that goes for me, too, Patricia," I said. "Please don't hesitate to call if I can help you with funeral arrangements, or anything else."

"You're both very kind," she said.

We went to the front door, opened it, and stepped out onto the porch. As Patricia was about to close the door behind us, she said wistfully, "Rory is dead. Hard to believe. I expect to see him walking in here any minute."

I swallowed the lump in my throat and managed a small smile. I was glad to see some sign that she'd recognized the grim reality of the situation.

Mort opened the front passenger door of his car for me, but I sensed that Robert was disappointed at being relegated to the rear.

"Perhaps you'd like to ride up front," I said.

My suggestion brought a hint of pleasure to his face.

Mort started to protest, but I said, "No, I'll be very comfortable in the back."

I was glad I made the decision to give up my front seat to Bob Brent. As we proceeded toward town, he became almost animated, questioning

Mort about the array of electronic communications gear wedged between the two front seats. Mort readily answered all the questions, and even demonstrated the use of the radio by calling headquarters. "This is Metzger," he said into the handheld phone. "On my way back in with Robert Brent. Should be there fifteen, twenty minutes. Over."

A voice came through the speaker. "Roger. I read."

"Over and out," Mort said. We both sensed that Robert would have liked to use the mobile phone, too, but Mort was not about to go that far.

As we pulled into the main part of Cabot Cove, Mort turned and asked, "Straight home, Mrs. F., or drop you some other place?"

"Home, if you don't mind."

As we approached the street on which I live, I noticed two cars parked in front of my house.

"Looks like you've got company," Mort said.

"Appears that way."

He turned into my driveway. I got out and came around to where Mort sat behind the wheel. He lowered his window. "Thanks for the ride," I said. I looked across to where Robert sat and said, "I'm very sorry about your father, Robert. Please tell your mother again to call if I can be of help."

His response was a glum nod and to turn away from me.

Strange young man, I thought as I approached

my front door. To my surprise, it opened, and I was greeted by Seth Hazlitt. Seth and I have keys to each other's houses and don't hesitate to make ourselves at home in either one.

"Hello," I said. "I thought you had a waiting room full of patients this afternoon."

"*Ayuh*, I did, but a couple of 'em canceled last minute."

As I stepped inside, I saw Cynthia Curtis, our head librarian and member of the town board, standing in the archway leading to my living room. "Hello, Cynthia. What a pleasant surprise."

"Seth insisted I come," she said. "I just put water up for tea. Hope that's all right."

"Sounds good to me," I said, hanging my coat up on a row of pegs and leading them into the living room. Seth had made a fire. I stood before it and rubbed my cold hands. "Feels wonderful," I said. I turned and asked, "What's up?"

Seth did the talking.

"Jessica, Cynthia came to me with a problem having to do with Rory Brent's murder."

I looked at Cynthia, a vivacious, energetic mover-and-shaker in the Cabot Cove community. "A problem concerning you, Cynthia?" I asked.

She looked to Seth to continue, which he did.

"It seems that everybody in town has already convicted Jake Walther of killin' Rory."

"That's terrible," I said. "How could people come to that conclusion so quickly?"

Now Cynthia spoke. "I suppose it's because of Jake's reputation, Jess. You know how it is. Doctors with a pleasant bedside manner get sued less than the arrogant ones."

We both looked at Seth. He smiled and said, "I certainly agree with that. Never been sued in my professional life, and proud of it."

"Jake has made so many enemies over the years," Cynthia said. "You know, he has that mean streak in him that seems to come out at the worse possible moments. I don't suppose there's anyone who's lived here for any length of time who hasn't been crossed by him. At any rate, all everyone is talking about is that Jake murdered Rory Brent."

I sat in a chair in front of the fireplace and looked into flames that were building. I understood her concern. Once a rumor gets legs, as they say, it's like the proverbial snowball rolling down hill. It suddenly struck me that Cynthia might be worried that townspeople would take matters into their own hands. I asked her if that was on her mind.

"Oh, no, I don't think so, Jess. People here aren't like that."

"You never know," Seth said sternly.

"Certainly not at this time of year," I said. "It's almost Christmas. Peace on earth. Goodwill toward men."

"And women," Cynthia added.

"And women," I said.

"You might be forgetting one thing," said Seth.

"What's that?" I asked.

"It wasn't just Rory Brent, a farmer, who's been killed. It was Santa Claus."

Initially, his comment struck me as funny. But it occurred to me just as quickly that there was a certain metaphorical truth to what he'd said. Rory Brent had become synonymous with Santa Claus in Cabot Cove. He was an icon, a man loved throughout the year, but revered once he donned his red Santa costume with its furry white trim, floppy red-and-white hat, and shiny black boots.

I stood and paced the room. "If what you say is true—and I agree there could be a problem having people running around already convicting Jake Walther—then what we have to do is come up with a quick plan to put it to rest. Any suggestions?"

"Maybe you should tell us what happened out at Rory's farm when you and Mort went out there," Seth said.

I thought for a moment, then said, "Well, there isn't much to say. The county police were there. It seems there's a little jurisdictional dispute between Mort and them. Patricia arrived while we were there. She was down visiting a cousin in Salem. She hadn't known about Rory's death. It wasn't pleasant being the ones to break the news. I came back in town with Mort and Robert Brent."

"You did?" said Cynthia.

"Yes. Mort wanted to interview him and thought headquarters was the best place to do it. He came readily enough."

"A bad seed, that boy," said Seth.

"Not terribly friendly, I agree, but I don't want to jump to conclusions about him the way you say others are ready to hang Jake Walther. Bob Brent has been telling Mort that he's convinced Jake killed his father. Not that that means anything. Mort asked him whether he had seen Jake do it, and Bob said he hadn't. He and Mort are at police headquarters as we speak."

"I was thinking of calling an emergency meeting of the town board," Cynthia said. "Make it an open meeting, invite the public. What do you think?"

I shrugged. "I'm not sure it would accomplish much, Cynthia. It might even fan the flames. Maybe it's better to let it settle down on its own."

"Seems to me the only thing will settle it down is if Mort's investigation rules out Jake," said Seth. "Until that happens, people will be looking at him like he's a murderer."

"Has anyone seen Jake since this happened?" I asked.

Seth and Cynthia shook their heads.

"I'm sure Mort will make interviewing Jake one of his top priorities, especially since Robert Brent is so adamant about pointing a finger at him. Maybe the best thing is to make Mort aware, if he isn't already, of the sentiment in town, and urge him to work as quickly as possible to either clear Jake or arrest him."

"Good suggestion," said Cynthia. "Would you call Mort?"

"Of course," I said. "Let me give him a little time with Bob Brent before I do."

Our conversation was interrupted by the whistling teakettle. After I'd served them and myself, I said, "Anything else on the agenda?"

"Matter of fact, there is," said Seth.

My arched eyebrows indicated I was waiting to hear what it was.

"We've got to decide who's going to play Santa Claus this year, now that Rory is gone."

"A good question," I said. "Any suggestions?"

"I've had some discussions with a few people from the festival committee," Cynthia said. "An interesting idea came up."

"I'm all ears," I said.

"You!"

I looked at Seth. "Me?"

"Interesting notion, wouldn't you agree?" Seth said. "Politically correct, as they say. Might be a real good thing for Cabot Cove to have the first woman Santa."

I couldn't help but guffaw. "That's ridiculous," I said. "Not the concept of having a woman as Santa Claus, but *this* woman? I hate to be vain, but I really don't think I look the part."

"That wouldn't be a problem," Cynthia said. "Always easy to make somebody look heavier than they are. You know, pillows strapped around the waist, that sort of thing."

"Absolutely not," I said. I glanced at Seth. "Have you ever considered being Santa Claus, Dr. Hazlitt?"

"No, and I don't intend to at this stage in my life. Too old to have all those little kids jumping up and down on my bad knees. You think about it, Jessica. Probably get us lots of media attention, having a female Santa and all. You know, television shows, maybe a reporter from a big paper. Would give everybody in Cabot Cove a boost."

"Well," I said, "I will not think any more about it because it is absurd. I think we're much better served focusing our attention on how to diffuse this situation concerning Jake Walther. There are many good candidates in this town for taking Rory's place as Santa. I'm not one of them. I'll call Mort as soon as you leave."

I didn't mean to say it in such a way that I wanted them out of the house, but I suppose it came off that way because they both stood, thanked me for the tea, and said they'd get back to me later after I'd had a chance to talk with Mort.

I was happy when they were gone, not because I didn't love being with them, but because it had been such a hectic, traumatic day. I needed some quiet time to think about what had transpired.

I made another cup of tea and went into my den that also serves as my writing room. I was between books, as they say, which was a pleasant change. Too often, I was facing deadlines around the holiday season, and swore every year I wouldn't allow it to happen. This time, things fell right, and I was free to enjoy the holidays.

I called Mort a half hour later and was told he'd returned to the Brent farm with Robert Brent. I left a message and decided to spend an hour catching up on correspondence I'd let slip over the past week. I'd just settled down to respond to a letter I'd received from an old friend and former mayor of Cabot Cove, Sybil Woodhouse, who'd moved earlier that year to California with her husband, Adrian, when I heard a knock at the door.

I glanced out my den window. I hadn't noticed that snow had now begun to fall with conviction, and a wind had picked up, sending the flakes swirling. A bad night to be out, I thought, as I got up from my writing desk and went to the front door, where I pulled aside a curtain on one of the side windows.

Standing there was Mary Walther, Jake Walther's wife.

Chapter Five

Mary Walther's arrival took me by surprise. I don't know how to explain it, but seeing her standing at my front door was unsettling. I suppose it had to do with the conversation I'd just had with Seth Hazlitt and Cynthia Curtis about Jake Walther and the rumor he'd murdered Rory Brent.

But as these thoughts went through my head, I had a parallel realization that I was being terribly rude. The weather outside had turned truly foul. There she was, standing in the snow and wind, while I peered through a window from the warm comfort of my home.

I opened the door. "Hello, Mary."

She didn't move, nor did her stern expression change.

"What a nice surprise," I said, standing back to allow her to enter. "Please, come in."

She looked as though she wasn't sure what to do next, but then entered the foyer. I closed the door behind her. "Can I take your coat and hat?" I asked, extending my hands.

"All right," she said. Large, thick fingers unbuttoned her plain gray gabardine coat. I helped slide it off her shoulders. She reached up and removed her artificial fur hat and handed it to me. I hung them on pegs and said, "Come in. I'll make tea. Unless you'd prefer coffee."

"Neither, thank you, Mrs. Fletcher."

I led her into the living room, aware of what a large woman she was. She stood six feet tall, and her body was boxlike, her face broad and square, too. Once, when I was in a shoe store, looking for winter boots, Mary came in looking for a new pair of moccasins. They had nothing in a woman's style large enough to fit her feet, which, I noticed, were measured at size twelve. She settled for a man's moccasin, saying as she paid at the counter, "Big feet, big heart, they say."

To which the sales clerk replied, "I'm sure that's true, Mrs. Walther. Have a nice day."

A big woman—everywhere.

I've always respected Mary Walther. Despite marriage to a difficult and unpopular man, she was active in the larger Cabot Cove community, quick to respond to charity events to help out someone who'd fallen on hard times. She was aware of the occasional snide, sometimes cruel comments behind her back, but seemed able to put them aside. Mary wasn't a leader; there always seem to be too many leaders and not enough soldiers to do the grunt work on a project. But you could depend upon her to follow through and get the job done.

Like Patricia Brent, Mary Walther married a farmer and lives on a farm. But there is a dramatic difference between both families.

While Rory Brent had been a successful farmer, Jake and Mary Walther seem always to be on the brink of insolvency. And the family's living arrangements are strange, to understate it. There isn't just one house on the property. There are three, each in decrepit condition and not larger than what might be termed a shack. The three houses are lined up one behind the other, starting a dozen or so feet from the road. Jake Walther, at least according to those who claim to know, lives in the house closest to the road. Mary lives in the next house up the hill, perhaps 200 feet from the first, with their only child, Jill, who was away at school. And in the third house lives Mary's mildly retarded young brother, Dennis, a sweet, pleasant man who earns his keep by helping Jake on the farm. I can't attest to it from personal knowledge, but people say that Mary would ring a bell just outside her door at mealtimes, and Jake and her brother would come to her house for breakfast, lunch, and dinner, then return to their respective houses.

Unconventional? Without a doubt. Then again,

there are undoubtedly those families who live in the same house without having any interaction. The older I get, the less critical I'm determined to be.

A number of merchants in Cabot Cove had complained about not being paid by Jake and Mary, and a few had taken legal action against them. The bank, I'd heard, had been threatening for a long time to repossess their farm and home.

The problem is, as Cynthia Curtis had put it, unpleasant people are sued more often than pleasant ones. Compounding the Walther's financial problems is Jake Walther's sour, combative personality. He is a tall, thin man with a craggy face and salt-and-pepper hair that looks as though it hasn't been combed in years. His clothing is always dirty and in need of repair, and his face is set in a perpetual scowl, to the extent that children express fear of him just because of the way he looks.

Mary sat ramrod straight in a chair I indicated, clasped her gnarled hands in her lap, and planted her feet firmly on the floor.

"Sure you don't want something?" I asked. "Perhaps some wine?"

"No, thank you, Mrs. Fletcher. I'm afraid this is not a social visit."

"Please call me Jessica," I said. "We know each other well enough for that."

Mary Walther and I established a bond of sorts

two years ago when her daughter, Jill, was about to graduate from high school. I'd taught a workshop that spring for students who'd achieved honor status in their senior English class, and Jill Walther was one of them. She was a shy girl, with a head of frizzy hair and who wore very thick glasses. When I read her first short story, I was immensely impressed with her talent and insight. This was a young woman who was definitely college potential, and who could, if she followed the right path, become a fine writer.

I encouraged her; she seemed to respond to my praise. One day she lingered after class, and we had a chance to discuss her future. She wanted to go to college, but her father didn't have the money to send her. Although she didn't state it, I sensed that even if Jake Walther had the funds to pay for her college education, he wouldn't do it.

I decided to help. I wrote to the dean of creative writing at New York University, where I'd taught on occasion, sent him copies of Jill's stories, and urged him to consider a full scholarship for her. He came through. Jill was thrilled at the news, although her father's reaction was not as positive. Eventually, Mary Walther managed to choreograph things so that Jill could go off to New York City and begin her college studies. She kept in touch through letters, and whenever she was home made it a point to visit me.

Mary Walther, not a terribly demonstrative person, was relatively lavish in her gratitude to me, and we'd maintained that good relationship ever since, not a close friendship by any means, but a warm feeling for each other.

"Not a social visit?" I said, taking a chair across from her and leaning forward to indicate my interest in what she was about to say. When she didn't speak, I said, "Would I be correct in assuming you're here because of what happened to Rory Brent?"

She closed her eyes for a second, opened them, and said, "Yes."

"Well, suppose you tell me what's on your mind."

She said flatly, "I'm afraid there is going to be big trouble."

I sat back and sighed. "Oh, I'm sure there will be. We don't have many murders here in Cabot Cove. My hope is that Rory was killed by someone passing through, not anyone who lives here."

"They're saying Jake did it," she said in that same low voice bordering on masculine.

"Yes, I've heard the rumor. People shouldn't jump to such conclusions."

"Jake isn't much liked in these parts," she said.

I wasn't quite sure how to respond. "I suppose people consider him to be . . . well, consider him to be a little angry at times."

"People don't give him a fair chance to be liked," she said.

I didn't necessarily agree with her, but didn't want to get into a debate.

She continued. "Jake's always been a hardworking man, Mrs. Fletcher. Hard work and not much to show for it. He gets bitter at times, mad at what the good Lord has dealt him."

I thought of other people I knew who'd been dealt a losing hand in life, too, but who, if they were bitter, didn't wear it on their sleeve the way Jake Walther did.

"Jake can be down right *jo-jezzly* at times. I wouldn't deny that."

Jo-jezzly was a popular Maine term for someone who was ornery or cussed. It seemed an apt description of Jake Walther.

"Not always easy living with him. I would say that for certain."

"Mary, you said there was going to be big trouble. Do you want to explain that a little further?"

She replied, "Jake knows what folks are saying about him and Rory, that they didn't get along and that Jake was the one who shot him. Jake says nobody is going to take him away from the farm because he didn't do anything wrong. He didn't, Mrs. Fletcher, I can swear to that."

I didn't know how she could be so certain, but decided that was something for Mort Metzger to examine.

"Mary, you say Jake won't allow anyone to take

him away from the farm. Do you mean he won't subject himself to questioning by Sheriff Metzger?"

Now she showed her first sign of animation. "Mrs. Fletcher, Jake's back at the house, got the door locked. He won't talk to anyone, not me, not Dennis. All he says over and over through the door is that nobody's going to take him away."

"Doesn't he realize that if he didn't kill Rory, he has nothing to fear from Sheriff Metzger or anyone else?" I asked. "All the sheriff would want to do is ask him some questions. Maybe he has an alibi, someone who can say he wasn't anywhere near Rory's farm this morning. But if he refuses to cooperate, he'll end up in terrible trouble that he doesn't deserve."

"Exactly, Mrs. Fletcher. That's the big trouble I was talking about. I can't talk sense to him. I tried. Had Dennis try, too, but he runs us off his part of the farm. I don't know what to do. I surely don't."

I thought for a moment before saying, "My only suggestion would be to go to Sheriff Metzger, tell him the situation, and see what he suggests."

She slowly shook her head. "Jake won't talk to the sheriff. But maybe he'd talk to you."

"Me? Why me? I don't have any relationship with your husband."

"Jake read all about how you saved Jed and Alicia Richardson over in London. Read it in the paper and saw it on TV. He was real impressed. Said you were a brave and decent woman."

I had to stop and think for a moment to sort out what she'd said.

A year or so ago I'd traveled to England and Scotland with a contingent of friends from Cabot Cove. The trip had been arranged by my dear friend, George Sutherland, a chief inspector with Scotland Yard in London, whose family had come from Wick, Scotland. He still owns the family mansion there, used most of the year as a hotel for tourists. He insisted I visit his homestead. When I told him I was making the trip with a number of friends, he said that wasn't a problem because he would simply close the hotel for the week we were there and accommodate everyone.

We started the trip in London, where I had a few days' business to attend to before heading north. While in London, Jed Richardson, who owns Jed's Flying Service, a two-plane airline operating out of Cabot Cove, and his new wife, Alicia, were abducted by a madman and held hostage in the infamous Tower of London. I ended up negotiating their release. I hadn't planned on doing that, nor did I aspire to the task. It just seemed to evolve into that situation. The London press played it up big, and it eventually found considerable space in American newspapers.

"Mary," I said, "that was a very unique circumstance. I'm not a negotiator and don't pretend to be. As a matter of fact, I don't *want* to be in that role. I don't think I would have any influence on your husband."

Her expression seemed to soften as she said, "I know I'm imposing, Mrs. Fletcher."

"Jessica."

"Jessica. I'm not the sort of person who imposes on other people. I think you know that. I guess because you're the sort of woman who's always ready to help others in trouble, I figured you'd help out in this situation. I guess I was wrong." She stood.

I, too, stood. "Mary," I said, "of course I want to help you and Jake. As a matter of fact, if there is the sort of trouble you're indicating, I would want to do anything in my power to head it off. But I can't do it unilaterally. I can't do this alone. It would be taking the law into my own hands, something I am firmly opposed to. If you really think I could be instrumental in convincing Jake to cooperate in the investigation, I'll be happy to do it, but only in conjunction with Sheriff Metzger and his department. I'm waiting for a call from him now, as a matter of fact. If you agree, I'll tell him the situation and suggest we all go together to talk to Jake. That's the only way I can be involved."

"I'm just afraid, Mrs. Fletcher, that if Jake sees the sheriff and his car, he'll do something crazy."

"Maybe I can convince Sheriff Metzger to use

a plain car, and to stay out of sight until I've had a chance to talk to Jake. Frankly, I don't think this will work. There is no reason for your husband to trust me, or to listen to my advice."

"But maybe he will. I know one thing for certain, Mrs. Fletcher."

"What's that?"

"He sure won't listen to me or anybody else I can think of."

Chapter Six

Mary Walther wasn't gone more than a minute when Mort Metzger returned my call.

"How did it go with Robert Brent?" I asked.

"All right, I suppose, although he's a strange young fella. Didn't have much to say except for repeating over and over that Jake Walther killed his father."

"Did he offer anything tangible to support that claim?"

"No, he did not. Well, maybe he did in a way. He said his father and Jake had a real altercation about a month ago or so. He says Jake came to the farm and confronted his father over something having to do with land and money. The kid says he didn't know the details of what the argument was about, just that Jake threatened to kill Rory. Said he'd be back to 'blow his brains out.'"

"That's something tangible, I would say. A direct threat of bodily harm."

"True, provided you believe what young Robert says. I'm not sure I do."

"Based upon what?"

"Based upon . . . well, gut instinct. You do what I do long enough and you develop a pretty good sense of whether people are tellin' you the truth or not."

"I wouldn't argue with that. Mort, Mary Walther just left my house."

"She did?"

"Yes. She was very distraught when she arrived. She's afraid that something really bad is going to happen because of the rumors about Jake having killed Rory. She told me Jake has holed up in his house on the property. He won't talk to her brother or Mary. Poor thing, it must be so difficult for her being married to Jake. I've always admired her determination to become involved in the community while knowing what people in town are saying about him."

"A good woman, Mary Walther," Mort said. "Sounds like Jake is actin' like a damn fool."

"Sounds that way to me, too. I told her I'd get your advice on what to do."

"Doesn't seem to be much question about what to do," he said. "Because of Robert Brent's accusation, my next move is to go out there and talk to Jake. But I sure don't want to walk into a war."

"No one wants that," I said. "I assume you intend to call the house before going."

"Sure, except the only phone is in Mary's house in the middle. You know that setup out there. She lives in the middle house—more like a shack, it seems to me—Jake lives in the one by the road, and her brother lives up the hill in the third house. Calling out there will just reach Mary. And if Jake won't talk to Mary or Dennis, doesn't seem I have much chance to reason with him except in person."

I asked, "Did Jake have any friends in town, Mort? Anyone he spent time with, trusted, maybe would confide in?"

There was silence while he pondered my question. Finally, he said, "None I can think of, Mrs. F., 'cept for maybe Doc Hazlitt."

"Seth? I didn't know Seth was friendly with Jake Walther."

"He's not. But Jake had a couple of medical problems over the last few months and went to Seth for treatment. From what I hear, Jake was pretty pleased with the way Seth handled things. Somebody told me—I can't remember who—that Jake said Seth was probably the only honest doctor in Maine. I don't think Seth charged him, at least not much."

"Then maybe Seth would have success talking sense to Jake, to get him to realize that the only sensible course is to cooperate with you, answer your questions, and put to rest any accusations that he killed Rory. Provided, of course, that he didn't."

"Maybe you're right, Mrs. F. I'll call Seth and run it by him, see if he'll come out to Jake's place with me."

"Good idea," I said. "If Seth agrees, would you have any objection to my coming along?"

"I don't see any," Mort said. "You might be helpful, considering Mary Walther came to you."

"I'll be waiting for your call."

I heard from him five minutes later. "I got hold of Seth just as he was leavin'. Told him the situation. He says he didn't charge Jake for treating him because he knew he was down on his luck and didn't have any money to speak of. Jake seemed real appreciative, according to Seth."

"Did Seth agree to go out to Jake's house with you?"

"*Ayuh.* He suggested we not go in my car. Might set Jake on edge. We'll go in Seth's."

"That makes sense," I said. "You'll pick me up?"

"Be there in a half hour."

Seth pulled into my driveway exactly thirty minutes later. By then it had really begun to snow, the flakes big and wet and sticking to the ground. At least the wind had abated, lessening the effect of the cold.

I got in the backseat and we headed for Jake Walther's farm.

"Seems to me an unusual way for the sheriff to interrogate a witness," Seth said grumpily, both hands on the wheel, eyes focused straight ahead.

"No rule about how I approach a suspect in a murder," Mort replied from the front passenger seat. He'd pulled his Stetson down low over his eyes and tucked his chin against his chest. "Seems to me we're doing it exactly the right way, considering what might happen if I did it by the book. No sense adding to the problems of having a leading citizen murdered here in Cabot Cove by ending up in some stupid standoff. Better to try and get Jake to cooperate. I'd hate to have to go out there, guns drawn, and drag him off. More people might get hurt."

"I think you're right," I said from the backseat. "The impact of Rory's murder is just really settling in on me. These kinds of things just don't happen in Cabot Cove, especially at Christmas."

Seth grimly reminded me of a couple of other murders that had occurred in our idyllic Maine town, although they had happened a number of years ago.

"Now tell me, Morton, how you want me to proceed with this," Seth asked.

"Depends on how brave you are, Doc."

Seth glanced over at the sheriff. "What in hell do you mean by that?"

"Well, according to Mrs. F., seeing me will only set Jake off, and we sure wouldn't want to send *her* up there to knock on the door. The way I figure it, we'll park out on the road a little bit away from the house. You'll go up to the door and tell Jake who you are and why you're there."

I leaned forward and placed my hands on Seth's shoulders. "That could be dangerous," I said. "If Jake is in as tormented a state of mind as Mary says he is, he's liable to panic. He might have guns with him."

"Somehow, no matter how mean-spirited Jake Walther is, I just can't see him shooting anybody," said Seth. "I don't think I'll have a problem getting him to talk to me. He's one of those fellas who's got a gruff exterior, but down deep there lurks a decent person. At least, that's the way I read him."

"What kind of medical problems did he have?" I asked.

"Can't discuss that," Seth said. "Doctor-patient privilege."

I didn't press him, but he volunteered, "Man has wicked arthritis. Neck, shoulders, hands, back. In lots of pain. Maybe that's why he's so *jo-jeezly* all the time."

I silently thought that Seth was probably right, and felt a twinge of compassion for Jake.

As we approached the Walther property, Seth slowed down, eventually stopping fifty yards from a narrow, rutted dirt driveway leading up past the three separate houses.

"Might as well get to it," Seth said, shutting off the lights and engine.

"I don't like this," I said. "I think we should go with you."

"But if Jake sees me, he might—"

I interrupted Mort. "I don't think Seth should simply go up there by himself, Mort. If the three of us go up, we'll have each other to lean on. You and I can stay back and let Seth do all the talking. If he's successful, and Jake opens the door, then you'll be right there to take advantage of it."

Mort chewed his cheek while he thought. He turned to Seth and asked, "What do you think?"

"Jessica is probably right," Seth said. "Of course, I don't mind goin' up there alone. But maybe we should be together. If I get him to cooperate, no sense having to come back down here and bring you up. Besides, if I'm going to stand out in the cold, you might as well, too."

I didn't think that was a particularly good reason for us to accompany Seth, but didn't express it. We got out of the car, slowly walked down the road to where the driveway intercepted it, and looked up at the first house where Jake lived. It wasn't much of a house, nor were the other two.

"Here we go," said Seth, leading us up the driveway. We reached a stone path that twisted up to the front of Jake's house, we took it, but paused at the two small wooden steps leading up to the porch.

Mort whispered, "Jess and me will stand over there on the porch while you talk to him through the door."

"*Ayuh,*" said Seth. He drew a deep breath; his lips were pressed tightly together. I said a silent prayer that this wouldn't backfire. Bad enough Rory Brent was dead without having someone else fall victim to violence.

We stepped quietly up onto the porch. Mort and I moved to our right, approximately six feet from the door. Seth knocked. There was no response. He knocked again. This time Jake Walther's raspy voice growled, "Who the hell is it?"

"Doc Hazlitt," Seth said loudly.

"What the hell are you doing here?" Jake asked. We judged he'd moved closer to the door because his voice had grown louder.

"Want to talk to you," said Seth.

Jake said, "Talk to me? About what?"

"About . . . about what happened to Rory Brent."

Silence.

"Jake, you listen to me," Seth said. "Folks in town are saying you had a spat with Rory, a pretty serious one, and some of 'em are even saying you might have shot him. Now I know you didn't shoot him, and the best way to make that point with everybody is for you to sit down with Sheriff Metzger, answer his questions, and put it to rest."

"Can't do that," Jake said.

"Why not?"

" 'Cause nobody'll believe me. Nobody ever does in this town. People would just as soon hang me and get it over with."

"Now, Jake, that's nonsense. Don't you trust me? You said you did."

"As a medicine man? Sure. Best damn doctor I've ever known, only I don't know many. But that's just you, Doc. Others in town got their own agenda, and it includes getting rid of me."

Seth looked to where we stood, our eyes open wide. I noticed Mort had unzipped his jacket and had rested his hand loosely on a holstered handgun on his right hip.

Seth said, "You can trust me, Jake, with anything, not just medicine. My word is good. You'd better believe that."

Jake didn't respond.

"You hear me, Jake? I'm telling you that nobody is going to do anything to you just because they don't like you. That's not the way things work in this country, certainly not in Cabot Cove. Sheriff Metzger doesn't think you killed Rory, but he has a job to do. He has to ask questions, and you're one of the persons he's gotta ask 'em of. I assure you all that will happen is that you and the sheriff will sit down, he'll ask his questions, you'll answer them truthfully, and that will be the end of it."

Unless he did shoot Rory Brent, I thought.

Walther responded, "Can't trust nobody in this town. Nope, can't trust nobody."

Seth tried another tack. "Your wife is right worried," he said. "She came to see Jessica Fletcher earlier tonight, told her how worried she was about you. You don't want to cause trouble for her and Jill, do you?"

"Mary had no right goin' to nobody."

"Not true," said Seth. "Mary is a good woman. Thought she was doing the right thing."

"You talked to Mrs. Fletcher?" Jake asked through the closed door.

"*Ayuh*," said Seth. "She's with me right now, on the porch."

That bit of news seemed to stun Jake into another moment of prolonged silence. He eventually asked, "Who else is with you?"

I knew the internal debate going on within Seth. Does he tell Jake that the sheriff is there on his porch, or does he lie and hope to get Jake to expose himself so that Mort could act. I knew the answer. Seth would not lie.

"I've got Mrs. Fletcher and Sheriff Metzger here with me on the porch, Jake. Now it's getting pretty damn cold out here. If I get sick, other people aren't going to get treated, and that'll be on your shoulders. If you give me pneumonia, I'm not sure I'll ever forgive you. Now open the door and let us in."

During the dialogue through the closed door,

the wind had picked up and the temperature seemed to have dropped twenty degrees. My feet were numb and my ears stung. I hoped it would quickly be resolved one way or the other. Either Seth would prevail and Jake would do as he was told, or the standoff would continue. If that happened, it would be up to Mort to take the next step, and I dreaded what that might be.

Suddenly, the sound of a bolt being lifted from a latch was heard from inside the house. Slowly, the door swung open, and Seth was face-to-face through a torn screen door with Jake Walther.

" 'Evening, Jake," Seth said. "I wouldn't mind if you'd invite us in."

Jake undid a hook and eye on the inside of the screen door and pushed it open. Seth motioned to us with his head, and we followed. It was a sparsely furnished room filled with clutter. Piles of old newspapers almost reached a low ceiling along one side. The only heat came from a wood-stove in another corner. The floor was bare wood and sticky. A small table by a window contained what looked like the remnants of a number of meals, empty open cans of pork and beans the primary cuisine. Also on the table was a handgun.

It worked, I thought as Mort, who was the last one into the room, closed the inside door behind us. I looked at Jake Walther, the top of his head almost touching the ceiling. He was dressed in bib overalls over a black flannel shirt. He hadn't shaved in days, and there was a crazed look in his large, watery, pale blue eyes.

Still, I didn't feel any sense of danger until I moved aside, affording Jake his first clear view of Mort Metzger. Mort had left his jacket open, and his hand continued to rest on his revolver. Jake scowled, grunted, mumbled an obscenity, and made a quick move to the table where his hand-gun rested. Mort was quicker. He pushed Walther against the wall, drew his weapon, and placed it against the back of Jake's neck. "Now don't do anything foolish, Jake Walther," Mort said. "Don't make things worse than they are."

It happened so fast that I didn't have a chance to react. But now my breath came in hurried spurts, and I backed away as far as I could from the confrontation.

Jake didn't resist as Mort deftly slipped a pair of handcuffs from his belt and secured them to Jake's wrists behind his back. That completed, Mort stepped back, allowing Jake to turn and face us. He looked directly at Seth and said, "Should have known not to trust anybody, including you."

"Damn fool thing you did, making a move for that gun," Seth said. "Nobody was here to arrest you. Mort just wanted to talk to you, but you pull a dumb stunt like that."

Jake looked at Mort. "Am I under arrest?" he asked.

"Depends," Mort said. "Doc is right. If you

hadn't made that move, we'd just be sitting around talking like friends and neighbors. You didn't leave me any choice. Now we're going to go downtown and leave that weapon behind. I assume you've got a proper permit for it. Once we get to my office, depending upon how you act and talk, I might just take those cuffs off and have that friendly chat I intended to have when I came here. Understand?"

Jake said nothing, simply looked at the floor as he leaned against a wall.

I motioned for Mort and Seth to come to where I stood. "Maybe I'd better go up and tell Mary what's happened."

"Good idea," Seth said, then turned to Mort. "I don't think it's a good idea to bring him downtown in my car. Should be an official vehicle."

"Right you are," Mort said. "Mrs. F., there's a phone up in Mary's place. Give a call to my office and tell whoever answers to send a squad car up here on the double."

I left Jake's house, went up the driveway to the middle dwelling, and knocked on the door. Mary Walther answered. "What are you doing here?" she asked.

I explained what had happened.

"Jake isn't hurt, is he?"

"No, but he made a sudden move that caused the sheriff to react. He had to put handcuffs on Jake and is taking him to headquarters to interview him about Rory's murder. I'm sure everything will be fine. I have to call the sheriff's office to have a car brought up here to take Jake into town. May I use your phone?"

A half hour later, Jake was in the backseat of a squad car driven by one of Mort's deputies. Mort got in the passenger seat, and Seth and I watched them drive off from Jake's front porch. Mary Walther had joined us.

"Will he have to stay in jail tonight?" Mary asked.

"No tellin'," Seth replied. "We'll just have to wait and see."

"I should be with him," Mary said.

The woman's loyalty to her husband was admirable, especially since it was pretty well known he didn't treat her with much kindness.

"No, you stay here," I said. "Is your brother up in the other house?"

"Yes."

"Maybe you should have him come down and stay with you tonight."

"I don't know if he will," she said.

"Well, give it a try," Seth said. "Ready to go back, Jessica?"

"Yes."

Before we left the porch, I looked deeply into Mary's eyes. There was profound sadness in them, and I wanted to wrap my arms about her and hug her. Which I did. Seth and I then drove back into town in relative silence.

"Come in for a drink, cup of tea?" I asked as we pulled into my driveway.

"Another time, Jessica. Didn't think I'd end up spending today the way we did."

"Nor did I. Do you have the same feeling I have, Seth, that Rory's murder is only the beginning of something worse about to happen in Cabot Cove?"

He thought it over before saying, "Matter of fact, I do. But let's not dwell on it. Good night, Jessica. Give me a call in the morning."

I felt deflated and fatigued as I approached my front door. It had been an unfortunate day, certainly one I never dreamed would occur when I got up that morning and prepared to go about my daily life.

It wasn't until I was only a few feet from the door and was about to insert my key that I noticed the large, circular green wreath with a puffy red ribbon hanging from it. I'd forgotten; the man who cut my lawn, shoveled my walk, and did minor repairs to my house always hung a wreath on my door in early December. Usually, the sight of it caused me to break into a smile. But I didn't smile this time. As pretty and symbolic as the wreath was, it only reminded me that this was shaping up to be a Christmas like no other I'd ever experienced.

Chapter Seven

My clock radio went off at seven the next morning, as it always did. I kept it tuned to Cabot Cove's only radio station, owned and operated by friends of mine, Peter and Roberta Walters. Pete did the morning show himself, weaving in interesting, often amusing tidbits of local news with pleasant music that reflected his own taste—and mine—mostly big band music and singers like Sinatra and Bennett, Mel Torme and Ella Fitzgerald.

But this morning I was awakened to the strains of "Have Yourself a Merry Little Christmas." I stayed in bed until the song ended. Pete came on with his deep, pleasant voice and said, "Good morning Cabot Coveites. This is your humble morning host reminding you that you have twenty-three shopping days until Christmas."

That reality caused me to sit up straight. Christmas seemed to start earlier and earlier each year, usually right after Thanksgiving, but even earlier in some instances. I wasn't sure I liked that, but since there was nothing I could do about it, I didn't dwell upon it.

I got up, put on slippers and robe, and went to the kitchen, where I turned on the teakettle and retrieved from a bag a cinnamon bun I'd bought the day before at Charlene Sassi's bakery. As I waited for the water to boil, I looked out my window at the rear patio, covered by what I estimated to be three inches of snow. You get good at judging the depth of snow after living in Maine for a while. The two bird feeders I'd hung near the window were doing a landslide business, my little feathered friends fluttering about them in a feeding frenzy.

The teakettle's whistle interrupted my reverie. Armed with a steaming mug of tea and the cinnamon bun, I went to the living room and turned on the television. The *Today Show* was on; the guest was an economist forecasting how well merchants would do this holiday season. I wasn't interested in that, so I shut it off and returned to the kitchen for the more esthetic show being put on by the birds. But as I watched them, thoughts of Jake Walther and what had occurred at his house last night took center-stage.

Judging from the way things had gone, my assumption was that Jake had been detained, at least overnight, in Mort Metzger's four-cell jail, which he was fond of referring to as his "Motel

Four," the humor undoubtedly lost on those forced to spend a night there.

I also thought of Mary Walther, poor thing, having to face what had become the town's apparent consensus that her husband had murdered Rory Brent. I desperately hoped it wasn't the case, that whoever shot Rory was a stranger passing through, a demented, vile individual who had no connection to Cabot Cove. But I had to admit that Jake's sudden move toward his weapon caused me to wonder whether there might be some validity to the rumor that there was bad blood between them, and that he'd killed Rory because of it. The contemplation made me shudder.

Our local newspaper was on the front steps. I brought it inside, made a second cup of tea, and read the paper from cover to cover. Originally, it had been a weekly. But the town had grown sufficiently to prompt its publisher to turn it into a daily paper, usually dominated by news of births and deaths, local events, and the goings-on of various citizens, but with an impressive national and international section culled from wire services to which the paper subscribed. Plans for the Christmas festival occupied two entire inside pages. Rory's murder took up most of the front page.

The reporter had tried to interview Mort Metzger, but our sheriff had simply replied, "No comment."

Good for him, I thought. What could he possibly say at this stage of the investigation?"

But a spokesman from county law enforcement was willing to speak, at length. I recognized the picture of the officer that accompanied the article. He'd been at Rory's barn when Mort and I arrived.

There was a biography of Rory, highlighting the fact that he'd played Santa Claus for our annual Christmas festival for the past fifteen years. A picture of him in his Santa costume was there, as well as a picture of his wife, Patricia. She, too, had decline to make a comment except to say that she was sad at her husband's death, and hoped that whoever did it would be caught quickly.

It was at the end of the article that speculation appeared about who might have killed Rory. The reporter mentioned that Robert Brent, son of the deceased, had volunteered to come to police headquarters to give a statement, and that Jake Walther, who'd been detained for questioning, was being held in the town jail. That bothered me. It would do nothing but give credence to the rumor that he was the murderer. We're innocent until proved guilty in court of law, but that doesn't necessarily apply to the court of human frailty and misconception.

I was tempted to try and reach Mort to get an update on what happened last night, but fought the temptation. It really wasn't my business, even though I'd been there when the incident with Walther had occurred. I showered and dressed. I had a nine o'clock meeting scheduled with Cynthia Curtis to discuss how we might approach the reading of Christmas stories to the children of Cabot Cove. She'd suggested the meeting when she left my house yesterday, and I'd agreed to it. She wanted Seth there, too, but he'd declined, claiming he had a busy patient load that morning.

It wasn't easy summoning enthusiasm for a meeting, which I assumed was the prevailing feeling of most people in town involved with the festival. Initially, learning of Rory's murder had put us all in shock. Now, twenty-four hours later, that shock had been replaced with a pervasive sense of gloom and depression.

But I knew that I, and anyone else, couldn't let that dominate our lives. The festival was too important to have it ruined by any single event, no matter how tragic it might have been.

Dimitri picked me up in his taxi at ten of nine and drove me to the library, where Cynthia waited in her office.

"Good morning, Cynthia."

"Good morning, Jess. Glad you could make it. Frankly, I wondered whether you'd show up."

"I said I would."

"Because of what happened yesterday. I didn't want to get out of bed this morning, I was so depressed over it."

I nodded. "I know exactly what you mean. But I reminded myself that we have a festival to put on. It might be rationalization on my part, but I think Rory would have wanted us to go forward."

"I agree. I got a call from Jim Shevlin this morning."

"How is our mayor?" I asked.

"Feeling pretty much the same as we do. He said he was going to meet with the festival committee at noon and suggest that the festival be officially dedicated to Rory's memory."

"That's a splendid idea."

She'd gotten up to greet me. Now she settled behind her desk, went through some papers, saying as she did, "At least having the murderer identified and under arrest might make things easier, provide some sort of closure."

"Pardon?"

She looked up. "Didn't you hear?"

"Hear what?"

"That Jake Walther is being charged with the murder of Rory Brent."

"No, I did not hear that."

"What have *you* heard?" she asked.

I recounted what happened the night before, and the circumstances under which Jake had been brought to police headquarters. When I finished, I added, "But Mort was simply going to question him. What happened? Did Jake confess to the murder?"

Cynthia shrugged and said, "I really don't know. You read the paper this morning?"

"Sure. But the article didn't indicate that Jake had been arrested, just that he had been detained for questioning."

"Mara says she got it from a good source that Jake is being accused of the murder."

I laughed. "The good old Cabot Cove grapevine at work, with Mara's Luncheonette as its headquarters. Mind if I use your phone?"

"Not at all."

I dialed the number for police headquarters. Deputy Tom Coleman answered, asked me to hold, and a minute later Mort came on the line.

"I was wondering when you'd get around to calling," he said.

"I wasn't going to. I didn't think it was my business. But I just heard that you're charging Jake Walther with Rory Brent's murder."

"Where did you hear that?"

"It came from . . . well, just a rumor floating around town."

"Damn Cabot Cove rumor mill," he said. "No. I had Tom drive Jake back to his house this morning. Kept him overnight and stayed up asking him questions. He admits he and Rory didn't get along. Maybe that's an understatement. But he swears he didn't kill him."

"Does he have an alibi?" I asked.

"Claims he does. Says he spent the morning fixing a crumbling stone wall with his wife's brother, Dennis."

"Believe him?" I asked.

"No reason not to, unless his alibi doesn't hold water. I was just about to go out to talk to Dennis when you called."

"Well, Mort, I'm glad the rumor doesn't have any foundation in fact. I'm with Cynthia Curtis. We're talking about the children's story program for the festival."

"Sounds like a good thing to be doing. I think Doc is a little upset at not having it all to himself again this year."

"Oh, is he? I certainly don't want that to be the case. I'd rather bow out than hurt his feelings."

"Don't give it a second thought, Mrs. F. You know Seth. Gets him self riled up over stupid things. Got to run. Talk with you later."

I hung up and told Cynthia what the true situation was with Jake Walther. When I finished, she asked, "What do you really think, Jess? You write about murders and have ended up solving some real ones."

"Too many real ones," I said. "I don't know what I think. What I'm determined to do is to not come to any conclusion until Mort and other investigators do their job."

"I wish you could instill that philosophy in everyone else in town."

"Well, maybe just expressing it to enough people will have that effect. Now let's get down to the business of the children's Christmas story hour."

Chapter Eight

My meeting with Cynthia lasted until ten. From the library I went directly to the office of my dentist, Anthony Colarusso, who was also president of the Cabot Cove Chamber of Commerce. Tony was not only a fine and caring dentist, he was an avid fisherman with whom I'd spent many pleasant mornings on some of the area's tranquil streams and rivers in search of elusive trout. We always fished with barbless hooks in order not to injure the fish we caught, enabling us to easily remove the hook from their mouths and send them back into the water for another day.

I didn't have a specific problem prompting me to make my 10:15 appointment, but a note on my calendar told me it was time for my semiannual checkup and cleaning. As usual, most of our conversation revolved around fishing, although the gauzy, metallic paraphernalia in my mouth kept the talk one-sided.

After agreeing we would be at a trout stream in the spring on the opening day of the fishing season, Tony said, "Shocking what happened to Rory Brent."

"It certainly was. Poor man. How could anyone do such a thing?"

"Rory was a patient. I always enjoyed it when he came in. Never had a bad word for anybody, always laughing and joking. I'm told Sheriff Metzger is focusing on Jake Walther as the most likely suspect."

It was inevitable, I suppose, that Jake Walther would be brought up in our conversation. I could only assume his name was being bandied about all over town that morning, as it had been since the earliest moments following the determination that Rory had not died of natural causes. Amazing, I thought, how scuttlebutt takes on a momentum of its own, the mere hint of an accusation mushrooming into the assumption of truth.

I said, "I just left Cynthia Curtis's office at the library, Tony, and spoke with Mort Metzger from there. He questioned Jake, but released him. Frankly, I hate to hear this kind of rumor circulating. The man is innocent until a court of law proves him guilty. At least that's the way the Constitution says it's supposed to be."

"Rinse," Tony said, indicating the basin next to the chair. I did as I was told.

"That's the problem when people create a negative reputation, like Jake. Easy to think the worst of somebody like that."

"I know exactly what you mean," I said. "Still . . ."

"I hear Jake has a good alibi."

I sat up a little straighter in my chair. "Who did you hear that from?"

"Susan Shevlin. She was in first thing this morning to have a filling replaced."

Susan Shevlin was married to Cabot Cove's mayor, Jim Shevlin, and operated the town's leading travel agency.

I shook my head as Tony removed the bib from around my neck. "My, how news gets around. She's right, though. Jake told Mort he spent the morning of Rory's murder fixing a stone wall with Mary Walther's brother, Dennis."

Tony's eyebrows went up. I knew what he was thinking, that Dennis Solten—Solten was Mary Walther's maiden name—might not be the best source of an alibi for someone accused of murder. Anyone who'd spent any time with Dennis knew that he was someone who agreed with anything and everything said, siding with totally opposing views as fast as they were proffered. Unlike his brother-in-law, Jake, who argued with everyone about everything , you never heard a word of disagreement from Dennis. The word "sweet" was most often applied to him. I sometimes wondered whether labeling him mildly retarded accurately reflected his situation. He had the look of a beaten puppy, someone who'd been put down so often in his life that it became second nature for him to be so malleable that he came off as intellectually slow, even dim-witted. Dennis Solten was as small as his sister was big. But he was a hard worker; no one would debate that. When he wasn't helping Jake on the farm, he hired out for yard work, snow shoveling, and other odd jobs. I'd hired him last fall to split two cords of wood from an ash that had died and fallen on my property. He attacked the task with vigor and dedication, swinging the heavy sledgehammer into the wedge he'd driven into each log with such energy that it tired me out just watching him.

"Are you saying that Dennis might be providing Jake with an alibi because Jake told him to?"

"Possibility, isn't it?" said Tony, stripping off latex gloves and tossing them into a special trash container. "Seems to me it wouldn't be hard to get Dennis to say almost anything."

I thought for a moment about what he said, then offered, "If that's true, then the opposite could occur. He could be persuaded to say something about Jake that would be incriminating."

"I guess it's a matter of who gets to him first with the most persuasive argument."

I left Dr. Colarusso's office, realizing how accurate his final comment had been. I also recognized that I, too, was feeding the Cabot Cove grapevine.

I wasn't doing it for the sake of gossip. At least I hoped it wouldn't be perceived that way. I made a few more stops before heading home for lunch, including the post office, the bookstore, where I'd promised to sign copies of my latest novel, and our local fish market to pick up a bushel of clams for steaming. Everywhere I went, the conversation quickly turned to Rory Brent's murder and the suspicion that Jake Walther had done the evil deed.

Happy to be home and away from the subject of murder and murderers, I placed water, two bay leaves, and a splash of white wine in the bottom of a very large lobster pot and put it on the stove. When it started to send up steam, I dumped in the clams. In the ten minutes it took for them to open, I melted some butter, cut off two pieces of crunchy French bread, and settled down at my kitchen table for one of my favorite meals. Although it had stopped snowing, it was still gray and raw outside, a perfect day to stay indoors. Unfortunately, I didn't have the luxury of spending the afternoon there. I was due at our local community college at three to meet with Bob Roark, dean of the creative writing department. He'd approached me a month ago to see whether I would be willing to teach a minicourse in mystery writing. Under ordinary circumstances, I would have had to decline his offer because of the press of my own writing schedule. But as it turned out,

I didn't plan to start my next book for at least three months, which gave me plenty of time to do those pleasurable things I too often never get around to. I enjoy teaching young writers, and have been doing more and more of it over the past few years, including New York University in Manhattan, and individual one-day seminars at other institutions of higher learning.

The clams were succulent—no surprise. After mopping up the last few drops of broth and butter with the final scrap of bread, I returned to correspondence I'd been working on the night before when Mary Walther's arrival had interrupted the process. I wrote letters until quarter of three, when Dimitri Cassis arrived with the taxi to take me to the college.

"What is new about Mr. Brent's murder, Mrs. Fletcher?" he asked once I'd gotten in the back-seat and closed the door.

"I really don't know, Dimitri."

"Did Mr. Walther do it?"

"Why do you ask that?"

"Everyone says he did."

"Well, Dimitri, just because everyone says so doesn't mean it's true. I don't think anyone knows who killed Rory Brent, although I certainly hope they find out as soon as possible."

He pulled out of my driveway, and we rode in silence for a minute before he said, "I don't like Mr. Walther."

"Have you had a problem with him?"

"Oh, yes. When I first came to Cabot Cove, I drove him to his house from town. He said he would go in the house and get money, but he never came out."

"That's not very nice," I said. "What did you do? Did you knock on his door?"

"No, Mrs. Fletcher, I did not think I could do that. I had only been here a few months, and had bought the taxi from Mr. Monroe two weeks before. I did not want to make trouble."

"Well, people should be paid when they provide a service. Is that the only time you were involved with Jake Walther?"

"Yes, ma'am, although I have seen him many times in the town. He's not nice to people."

"Yes, I know. He isn't very pleasant."

We said nothing else until Dimitri pulled up in front of the administration building on the community college campus.

"Put it on my bill," I said.

"Of course," he said. "You are my best customer."

"I'm glad to hear that."

"Mrs. Fletcher?"

"Yes?"

"I would not be surprised if Mr. Walther killed Mr. Brent."

"And I would be very sad."

He nodded and said, "I understand. You will call for me to pick you up?"

"Yes. It should be in about an hour."

I'd met Dean Robert Roark shortly after his arrival in Cabot Cove. He'd come to our community college from the English Department of Purdue University, where he'd been rated the department's most popular and effective teacher. Having been born in Maine played a major role in his decision to leave a comfortable Midwest teaching position to take over a department at a two-year community college. No matter what his motivation, he quickly became a valuable asset not only to the college, but to the community at large.

I judged him to be forty years old. He had long blond hair the consistency of corn silk, and was blessed with boundless energy and enthusiasm. My first experience with him was when he put together a conference featuring Maine writers. I remember distinctly being impressed with how many writers showed up. Maine certainly has its share of authors and journalists.

Since the conference, Dean Roark and I kept in touch, which led to his asking me to teach the course in mystery writing.

His office seemed to have boundless energy, too, if inanimate objects could generate that. Floor-to-ceiling shelves were crammed with books. Dozens of elaborately carved ducks, which he collected as a hobby, filled every space not occupied by a book. He wore a blue-and-white striped shirt, red-and-white suspenders, and a floppy yellow bowtie.

"Jessica, how wonderful of you to come. Right on time, I see, but that's no surprise. I've always suspected that mystery writers have to be punctual and organized."

I laughed. "Why would you assume that?"

"Because in order to write a good murder mystery, the writer has to have an organized mind to stay on plot, or else the reader is cheated. Don't you agree?"

"Well," I said, taking off my coat and tossing it on a chair piled with books, "I do tend to be a relatively neat and organized person, although I'm not sure that extends to my writing. At any rate, it's good to see you, too."

He realized I didn't have any place to sit and quickly emptied another chair of its books and file folders. "Tea?"

"That would be lovely, if it's no bother."

"No bother at all. Back in a jiffy."

He returned with two steaming mugs, handed me one, and settled behind his desk. "So, Jessica Fletcher, who killed Rory Brent?"

The bluntness of his question surprised me, and I didn't have a ready answer. I did say, "My guess is as good as yours, Bob, or anyone else's for that matter. A shocking event."

"Certainly was. I didn't know Mr. Brent, although I think I met him once or twice in passing. Seemed like a nice fellow. Played Santa Claus every year, didn't he?"

"Yes, and was wonderful at it. A shame you didn't know him better. He was a delightful man, not a mean bone in his body."

"A shame bad things always seem to happen to nice people."

I nodded.

"Lots of speculation in Cabot Cove about who killed him," he said.

There was no escaping it. Here I was for the purpose of discussing a class I would teach, and the conversation immediately went to Rory Brent's murder, and rumors floating around town about who did it.

"Do you know this Jake Walther fellow?"

"Yes, but not well. No one knew Jake very well because he preferred it that way. I know his wife a lot better."

"From what I hear, it's an open-and-shut case."

I looked at him skeptically. "I hardly think that, Bob. The man was questioned, but not arrested. He has an alibi."

"He does?"

"Yes. His wife's brother, who lives on the property with them."

"I hadn't heard that. Good for him. I mean, lucky for him to have an alibi."

I thought back to what Tony Colarusso had said

about Dennis Solten not being a terribly reliable alibi, and wondered what conclusion Mort had reached after speaking with him.

"I was thinking just before you arrived, Jessica, about the potency of rumor, especially where murder is concerned. Have you ever dealt with that in one of your books?"

I shook my head. "I've written so many I have trouble remembering specifics about some of the earlier ones. Yes, as a matter of fact I did deal with rumors in a small town. The rumor became so pervasive that an innocent man was charged with murder."

I hadn't thought about that book in connection with Rory Brent's murder. But now that I had, the entire plot, and many scenes dealing with it, came back to me.

"Ah ha," Bob said, sipping his tea. "You could have a situation here where fact follows fiction."

"I don't think one has anything to do with the other, except as a coincidence." I then decided I might as well ask, "What's the latest rumor you've heard?"

"Obviously, I'm not as up to speed as you are. I had no idea Mr. Walther had an alibi. What I heard was that he was taken into custody and retained overnight at the jail by Sheriff Metzger."

I thought back to the circumstances that led Mort to slap cuffs on Jake and bring him into town, but wasn't about to talk about it.

Bob said, "I've read a number of your books, as you know, but I don't recall the one you mentioned."

"Written a long time ago, early in my career," I said. "It was called . . . let me see . . . it was called *The Hanging Vine*. I think I originally called it *The Hanging Grapevine*, but my editor considered it awkward. He felt readers would get the connection without including the word 'grape' in it."

"I'll have to read it."

"I'll drop off a copy next time I'm here. So, Bob, tell me about this minicourse you want me to teach."

I called Dimitri Cassis forty-five minutes later and asked him to pick me up. Bob Roark walked me to the foyer of the administration building, where we chatted about the weather and the upcoming Christmas festival until Dimitri pulled up in his vintage station wagon.

"I'm excited about the course," I said, shaking Bob's hand.

"To have someone of your reputation teach at a community college is a real feather in the cap—a feather in *my* cap. I really appreciate it."

"What's the college doing concerning the festival?"

"Lots. Musical and theater groups putting on performances. Should be fun, although the murder of Santa Claus takes the edge off it."

"I know what you mean, but I'm determined it won't, if only out of deference to Rory's memory. He would have wanted the festival to go on as big and bright as ever."

The first thing I always do when entering my home is to check the answering machine. The little red light was blinking, indicating I had received a call. It turned out to be my publisher, Vaughan Buckley, calling from New York. His Buckley House had been publishing my novels for the past ten years, and I was one of those rare, it seems, writers who is blissfully happy with my publisher and the job it does publishing and marketing my books. Over those ten years, Vaughan and his wife, Olga, had become dear friends, and I often stayed with them in New York when visiting there. I returned his call immediately.

"Jessica, how are you?"

"Fine. I got your message. I was at a meeting. I'm going to teach a creative writing seminar at our local community college."

"Good for you. Keep your eyes open for the next John Grisham."

"I'll do my best. You called. How's Olga?"

"Tip-top."

"What's up?"

"A brilliant idea from your publisher."

I laughed. "One of many."

"I read about the murder of that farmer in your

town. His name—yes, here it is in the story, Rory Brent."

"A tragedy," I said. "He was a wonderful man, loved by all. He'd played Santa Claus at our annual Christmas festival for the past fifteen years."

"So the story indicates. That was the peg the writer hung the article on, that a beloved Santa had been gunned down in tranquil Cabot Cove, Maine."

"I didn't think it would interest the press outside of this area," I said.

"An AP story, out of Bangor. So, what's the latest on it?"

"No suspects," I said. "A few accusations, and many rumors, but no one arrested. At least as far as I know."

"Who's being accused?" Vaughan asked.

"A fellow named Jake Walther. Jake is another farmer. An unpleasant sort, not liked by many people in town. The deceased son claims Jake killed his father, but has nothing to support that. Sheriff Metzger interviewed Jake at length and released him. From what I hear, Jake has an alibi, and Mort was checking it today. I haven't heard how it came out."

"What's your take on it, Jess?"

"I don't have a take on it, Vaughan. Unfortunately, I got drawn in when Mort originally went out to talk to Jake. I'm friendly with Jake's wife, Mary, and she asked me to help. Jake was acting irrationally because he's convinced everyone believes he killed Rory, and no one will believe that he didn't. I suppose I can't blame him, although he's brought a lot of it on himself because of his sour disposition. As we say in Maine, he's 'some ugly.' "

Vaughan laughed. " 'Some ugly.' Certainly descriptive enough. You folks up there do have a knack for turning a phrase."

"On occasion. Frankly, Vaughan, I'm trying to put it out of my mind and focus on the upcoming holidays. I'm going to be reading Christmas stories to children as part of the festival. You remember my friend Dr. Seth Hazlitt?"

"Of course. How is he?"

"The same as always. He usually does the reading, but this year I'm going to share the stage with him. Should be fun."

I wish I could be there."

"You can, but hotel rooms are at a premium. You and Olga are always welcome at my place."

"I'll talk to her, maybe plan to come up for a few days."

"I'd love it. So, what's this brilliant idea you've come up with?"

"That you shelve plans for your next novel, and instead do a true crime book based upon this murder of Santa Claus."

"That never would have crossed my mind. I'm not a true crime writer."

"But you could be. It would be a nice change of pace, wouldn't it, dealing with fact rather than having to conjure up plots and characters? There they are, right in your lap. You know them, and you certainly know the setting in which this took place. Make a great book."

"I don't think so, Vaughan."

"Don't come to an instant decision. Promise me you'll think about it for a day or two. Readers love murder stories that take place in small towns, involving small-town people. People getting knocked off in big cities are a dime a dozen, but not when Santa is murdered three weeks before Christmas."

"I'll think about it only because the brilliant idea came from you. But don't count on it. Talk to Olga about coming up and spending a few days during the festival. You'll love it."

I spent the next hour bringing down Christmas decorations from the attic, where I keep them from year to year. Vaughan's call had reminded me that there were, indeed, only three weeks left until Christmas, which meant I'd better get busy writing cards, making a gift list and, in general, pulling myself together for the holiday season.

I was in the midst of reviewing my Christmas card list when Richard Koser called. Richard is a successful professional photographer who'd taken the photographs of me that appear on my book jackets. He and his wife, Mary Jane, are superb chefs, adventuresome kitchen partners whose culinary expertise range from Indian to Thai, Tex-Mex to down-home New England clambakes. Once, I attended a dinner party at their home, featuring an array of Indian foods—dishes like hommos bi tahini and chicken cous cous, and a dessert called galactaboureko—none of which pleased my pedestrian palate. I'm sure the food was superb, and my reaction was not intended to be judgmental. Richard and Mary Jane understood. "Indian dishes are an acquired taste," they had graciously said.

"Just as long as you invite me to other dinner parties that aren't Indian," I had said.

The one to which I'd been invited that evening would feature, according to Richard, an unusual approach to New England cooking, and I'd been looking forward to it since being invited two weeks ago. Besides excellent food, parties at the Koser home were always spirited and enjoyable.

"Just making sure you'll be coming tonight," Richard said.

"Absolutely," I said. "Who else will be there?"

"The familiar and the unfamiliar," he said, laughing. "My agent from Boston and his wife are in town and staying with us. Friends from New York are also up for a few days, staying at Jim Rich's Inn. Doc Hazlitt promised to come by, and Mort and his wife are joining the party."

"Mort? I'm surprised. I didn't think he had much time for socializing these days."

"Because of the Rory Brent murder?"

"Exactly." I tried to catch myself before asking the next question, but failed. "What do you hear about the murder, Richard?"

"Not very much. I've been holed up in my darkroom all day, except for a quick trip to the barber. Word there is that Jake Walther did it."

I quickly changed the subject. "What's this special approach to New England cooking we'll be enjoying tonight?"

Another laugh. "I want it to be a surprise. And no hommos bi tahini. That's a promise. Seven?"

"See you then."

Chapter Nine

Although I enjoy cooking, I would never claim to be a particularly successful or inventive chef. That's why I enjoy being around people who are, like Richard and Mary Jane Koser. For this particular evening, they'd used a recipe for baked oysters taken from a cookbook called *The Accomplished Cook: Or, The Art and Mystery of Cookery*, published in September of 1664, more than three hundred years ago. Pages from it had been reproduced verbatim in another book called *Maine Coastal Cooking*, published more recently by Down East Books, a Maine publisher.

Our hosts parboiled the oysters in their own juices, washed them in warm water, dried them, seasoned them with pepper, nutmeg, yolks of hard eggs, and salt, wrapped them in a wonderful homemade piecrust, and baked them in the oven. It was a superb entree; everything else served was on the same level of excellence.

Following dessert, we sat in the living room, where Richard served cordials. My antenna had been up during dinner to pick up any conversation about Rory Brent's murder, and the speculation that Jake Walther was the murderer. To everyone's credit, dinner-table conversation touched upon every subject except the murder.

But once in the living room, Seth Hazlitt raised it. "Well now, Morton," he said, "we've all been on our best behavior this evening."

"How so?" our sheriff said, sitting on a couch next to his wife.

"Not a word about Rory's murder. But I'll bet my bottom dollar that everyone here has a question for you."

Mort looked at me before saying, "I figure you're right, Seth, and I appreciate everybody holding their tongues. No sense asking me questions. I can't discuss an ongoing investigation."

"Who's Rory?" Richard's cousin asked.

"A local farmer who was murdered the other day," Seth said.

"Murdered?" the cousin said, looking at me. "I thought the only murders that happened in Cabot Cove were in your books, Jessica."

"Generally, you're right," I said, "but this time it was for real."

Richard's agent narrowed his eyes and said, "You didn't have anything to do with it, did you, Richard?"

"Me?"

"Sure. Remember the old radio series, 'Casey, Crime Photographer'?"

Seth laughed. "I'm the only one old enough here to remember it," he said. "Folks joked that it was called that because the way Casey took pictures, it *was* a crime."

"I never heard of it," the cousin said.

"You're investigating the murder?" the agent asked Mort, her eyes open wide.

"Afraid so," he replied.

"Has him out of the house day and night," Mort's wife said, patting her husband on the arm. "I prefer it when the only crime he has to investigate is somebody's lobster pot being stolen."

Although many questions were now asked of Mort, he remained adamant in his commitment not to discuss the Rory Brent murder. I admired him for that, although I admit my curiosity level wasn't exactly dormant.

The party broke up at eleven, late for midweek Cabot Cove social events. We tend to be early-to-bed, early-to-rise people. Seth drove me home.

"Come in for a nightcap?" I asked.

"*Ayuh,* don't mind if I do."

The oyster pie had left me thirsty, and I poured myself a club soda with lime. Seth readily accepted my offer of brandy.

"Pleasant evening," I said as we settled in the living room.

"Always is at Richard and Mary Jane's. Don't know if they're the best cooks in Cabot Cove, but they come close."

"I was proud of Mort this evening, not succumbing to the temptation to discuss Rory's murder."

"He is capable of keeping his mouth shut on occasion," he said, tasting the brandy and smacking his lips. "The perfect end to a nice evening."

"Seth, has Mort told *you* anything about going out to check on Jake's alibi with Dennis?"

He didn't answer, but his expression told me he had, indeed, been privy to additional information about the murder. I know Seth well enough not to press. If he wished to share it with me, he would.

"I spoke with Dr. Treyz this afternoon," he said, taking another taste of his brandy.

"Oh?"

"He finished up the autopsy on Rory."

Again, I didn't push for further details. You get from Seth Hazlitt only what he wishes to give you.

"*Ayuh,* told me it was a twenty-two that killed Rory. Bullet lodged right in his brain."

"I assume it was turned over to Mort," I said.

"I suspect it was. Probably go out to the state forensic lab down to Portland. It's official, Jessica. Somebody put a bullet in Rory Brent's head."

I felt a sudden chill, and eyed Seth's half-filled snifter of brandy. But I knew the shiver that went through me was not the result of the temperature in the room. Each time I thought of Rory Brent lying dead on the cold dirt floor of his barn, I suffered a physical reaction, as though someone had set off an electrical charge inside, or poked a knife in my ribs.

"Want some cookies?" I asked.

"Thank you, no, Jessica. Quite content."

I was heading for the kitchen to refill my glass when Seth said matter-of-factly, as though speaking to no one in particular, "Jake's alibi holds up."

I stopped midstride, turned, and looked at him. "Dennis corroborated what Jake said, that they were fixing a stone wall together?"

"That is correct," said Seth.

"I had my teeth cleaned this morning by Tony Colarusso. He questioned whether Dennis could be counted on as a reliable alibi."

"I suppose Tony is right, Jessica. But as far as Mort is concerned, Dennis gets Jake off the hook."

"Mort told you this himself?"

"That he did. 'Course, he only gave me a *scrid* of information. Just a wee bit."

"But important information, I'd say. Does this mean that Mort has officially ruled out Jake as a suspect?"

"Hard to say. I didn't get into that with him. And if I were runnin' the investigation, I'd be looking elsewhere. 'Course, I'm not runnin' the investigation."

He stood. "Much obliged for the brandy, Jessica. What's on your agenda tomorrow?"

I glanced at the grandfather clock in a corner of the room. It was a few minutes past midnight. "You mean what's on my agenda *today*? A busy schedule, but I won't bore you with the particulars. I'm sure we'll touch base again. Thanks for the ride, Seth. Careful home. Watch out for that black ice."

"*Ayuh,* I certainly will. Good night."

Although the hour was late, I wasn't tired, and sat up until after one thinking about what had occurred since that fateful morning of the Christmas festival planning meeting, when Tim Purdy arrived back from Rory Brent's farm with the grim news that he was dead. And then, of course, the tragedy was compounded after Mort visited the Brent farm and reported to us at lunch that it appeared Rory had been murdered.

Eventually, I climbed into bed and tried to read a few more pages in the book I'd started. But, as often happens, the act of reading quickly caused my eyes to lower. My final thought before I drifted off was the conversation I'd had with Vaughan Buckley about doing a true crime book based upon the Rory Brent murder. Doing such a book held little or no interest for me. But then again, maybe it wouldn't be such a bad idea to do a little poking around in the event I changed my mind.

I knew one thing for certain: I wanted Rory

Brent's murderer brought to justice before the Christmas festival. If it still hung over our heads during that joyous period of time, much of the Christmas spirit—and what it was supposed to mean—would be lost.

Peace on earth, goodwill toward men.

There would be no peace in Cabot Cove until Rory's murderer was behind bars.

Chapter Ten

I was up early the next morning and feeling remarkably refreshed, considering the late hour I'd gone to bed. Maybe it was the weather; the sun was shining brightly, and the sky was a deep, unblemished blue.

A perfect morning for a brisk walk, I thought as I prepared a simple breakfast, then took a shower. A half hour later, dressed in my favorite sweatsuit worn over a sweater, a scarf to keep my ears warm, and a new pair of expensive sneakers on my feet (*Why* are sneakers so expensive these days?), I headed out the front door and for town.

Because I'm as much a creature of habit as anyone else, I usually find my walks taking me in the same direction each time. Sometimes, when I think of it, I alter my route, if only to enjoy different scenery. But this morning I didn't bother being creative in choosing what streets to take. The only thing on my mind was to get moving, breathe in the cold, crisp air, and feel my blood flowing.

It takes only ten minutes to reach the center of Cabot Cove from my house. When I arrived there, I glanced at my watch. It was seven-thirty. Even at that early hour the main street—aptly named Main Street—was bustling. That is one of the reasons I enjoy taking morning walks into town. It's a chance to see friends before they become immersed in their work and daily lives.

I bumped into Sandy and Bernadette, who own the Animal Inn, a wonderful kennel where dogs and cats placed in their loving charge are treated royally.

"How are all your canine and feline borders?" I asked.

"Making the usual racket," said Sandy. "I think they sense Christmas is coming." To which Bernadette added, "A full house, no vacancies. Not an empty run in the place, and looks like it will stay that way right through the New Year."

"That's called prosperity," I said.

"I suppose you're right, Jess," Sandy said. "We've been turning down callers from miles away who want to bring their pets with them to the festival. Hate to say no but—"

I'd traveled another half block when I was stopped by Mickey and Joan Terzigni, on their way to open up their sign shop.

"Keeping busy?" I asked.

"With the Christmas festival coming up?"

Mickey said, laughing. "Can't keep up with all the signs the festival committee keeps ordering. You?"

"Not very busy at all," I said, "and loving every minute of it."

The only problem with running into so many people on my walk is that it interrupts the rhythm I try to establish, one that will benefit my cardio-vascular system.

I eventually left the downtown area and headed for the waterfront. The smell of sea air was bracing, the sound of gulls overhead providing what almost sounded like a choir—were they singing a Christmas song? I smiled at the thought.

The wind off the water was brisk, and I soon regretted not having dressed more warmly, perhaps adding a jacket over my sweatsuit. People were going in and out of Mara's Luncheonette, but I resisted the temptation to stop in for a cup of coffee and whatever caloric breakfast pastry she'd come up with that morning. After pausing on the dock to take in the stunning vista of sky and water, I went to the shore, removed my sneakers and socks, and walked barefoot along the water's edge. The sand was surprisingly warm on my bare feet, at least below the surface. Many people were on the beach, some throwing sticks for their dogs to fetch, others walking hand in hand. A man combed the sand with a metal detector in search of buried treasure. The sound of children's laughter rose above the steady slap and swish of waves breaking onshore.

At first, I wasn't sure I heard correctly. Had someone called my name? When I heard it a second time, I stopped and turned. Tom Coleman, Sheriff Metzger's deputy, was waving to me from where the sand ended at a series of large boulders, behind which was a parking lot.

"Good morning, Tom," I said when I reached him. "Beautiful day for December."

"Yes, ma'am, I suppose it is," he said. "The sheriff's been looking for you."

"Looking for me? Why?"

"Has to do with Jake Walther, I think."

"How so?" I asked, sitting on a rock, brushing the sand from my feet and between my toes, and putting on my socks and sneakers.

"He didn't really say, Mrs. Fletcher, except that Mrs. Walther is at headquarters. I think she's looking for you, too."

"Has something bad happened?" I asked.

"My car is right up here," was his reply.

I accepted his hand to help me up onto the rocks and followed him to his police cruiser.

Five minutes later I was in Sheriff Mort Metzger's office. Mary Walther stood by the window, her back to me.

"Good morning," I said.

"Good morning, Mrs. F.," said Mort.

"Good morning, Mary," I said.

She turned and looked at me with red-rimmed eyes.

"What's the matter?" I asked. "I assume it must be something important to have sent Tom down to the beach to interrupt my morning constitutional."

When Mary didn't respond, Mort said, "I arrested Jake this morning for Rory Brent's murder, Mrs. F."

Mary bit her lip and turned away again.

"What happened?" I asked. "I thought Jake had an alibi."

When neither of them responded, I added, "Didn't Dennis say he was fixing a stone wall with Jake the morning Rory was killed?"

"That's what he said the first time, Mrs. F., but I had my suspicions, so I went out there first thing this morning and talked to him again. Seems he's changed his story."

"He wasn't with Jake that morning?"

"Afraid not. Dennis says Jake told him to come up with that story so that he would have an alibi. But after a little prodding, I got the truth out of him."

I thought of Tony Colarusso's comment that Dennis would testify to anything, depending upon who was most persuasive. Was that the case here? Had Mort led Dennis into this total turnabout in his story?

Mary again faced me. "I'm afraid Dennis is telling the truth this time, Mrs. Fletcher."

"Please, it's Jessica."

"Jessica. He confided in me that he'd told the sheriff he'd been with Jake that morning only because he was afraid of Jake. No, Dennis was not with Jake when Rory Brent was killed. I know that for a fact. After all, he is my brother."

"But such a drastic change in story," I said, exhaling loudly. "And why would he be afraid of Jake? He's lived with you and Jake on the farm for many years."

"I know, I know," said Mary, slowly shaking her head and sinking into a chair. "But just because Dennis wasn't with Jake doesn't mean Jake killed Rory." Having stated that seemed to perk her up. She sat forward and looked at Mort. "It doesn't necessarily mean that, does it, Sheriff Metzger? I mean, just because he wasn't with Jake doesn't mean Jake killed anyone."

"I suppose that's what a jury will have to decide, Mrs. Walther," Mort said glumly. "All I know is I have enough to hold Jake on suspicion of murder until the D.A. decides whether to indict."

"Where is Jake?" I asked.

"In jail," Mort said.

"Why did you send for me?" I asked.

"Because I asked him to," Mary answered. "I don't know, Jessica, but sometimes I think you're the only real friend I have."

Her comment struck me as strange. Although we had been friendly, we'd never socialized the way true friends do, only interacted through mutual involvement in community activities. To call me her only friend was, in my judgment, a gross exaggeration.

Still, my heart went out to her. If she viewed me that way, it meant she harbored a terrible distrust of everyone else she'd gotten to know over the years.

"Mary, what would you like me to do?" I asked. "How can I help?"

Mort answered for her. "Jake's going to need a lawyer, Mrs. F. I told Mary that we could get him a public defender, but she said she wanted to talk to you first."

"Talk to *me* about lawyers?" I said.

"Because you seem to be the one person in Cabot Cove that everyone looks up to, Jessica," Mary said. "And I know you understand something about the legal system because of the books you write. Maybe I was out of place. I shouldn't have bothered you. It isn't your concern."

I pulled up a chair and patted her hand. "Mary, you haven't bothered me at all. I want to help. Mort is right. If you don't have the money to hire a lawyer, the state will provide a public defender."

"But that would be someone I don't know, that Jake doesn't even know. We don't have the money to pay an expensive lawyer, but I have some cash saved. Not a great deal, but maybe enough to use as a down payment. I could pay off a lawyer's fee over time. Jessica, all I want is to help Jake because I know he did not do this. He did not kill Rory Brent!"

Her voice had risen in volume, causing me to sit back, as though pushed by a hand. I looked to Mort, who continued to sit behind his desk, hands folded beneath his chin, eyes narrowed as he took in the conversation.

"How about Joe Turco?" I said.

"Who is he?" Mary asked.

"A wonderful young attorney who moved here only six months ago. He's a fine young man with excellent legal training, studied law in New Hampshire and New York City. Oxford, too, I think."

"Oxford, England?" Mort asked.

"Yes. He'd been practicing in Manhattan, and handling cases in New Hampshire, too. He's moved here because he likes to fish, and wanted a more quiet life than in Manhattan. He's building his practice. Would you like me to talk to him, see what he would charge to defend Jake?"

"Yes, of course," Mary said.

"It might not even involve much legal representation," I offered. "As of now, Jake hasn't been indicted." I turned to Mort. "That's correct, isn't it?"

"*Ayuh,*" he said.

"If Joe Turco is willing to take the case, he can handle this phase of things, maybe see that Jake is released on bail, something like that. I really don't know because I'm not a lawyer. But I have a lot of faith in this young attorney, who is now a member of our community, and I'd be happy to speak with him. I'll go see him when I leave here."

Mort said, "I'm not much of a fan of attorneys, as everybody knows, but I have got to admit I'm impressed with this young Turco fella. Got a nice way about him, which I can't say about most lawyers. It's a good suggestion Jessica is making, Mrs. Walther."

I stood. "Unless you want me here for something else, I'll go look him up right away."

Mary, too, stood, and took both my hands in her large ones. "God bless you, Jessica," she said. "I knew I could count on you. I don't know what I would do without you."

Again, this expression of friendship made me uncomfortable, although I understood that she was doing everything she could do to express her gratitude. I hadn't done anything yet, but I did feel my suggestion about Joseph Turco was a good one. What a terrible situation for anyone to be in, I thought as I picked up my scarf from where I'd laid it on the edge of Mort's desk, and wrapped it around my neck. I said to Mary, "Will you be home after you leave here?"

"Yes. I have nowhere else to go."

"Don't give up hope, Mary," I said. "I'm sure things will work out."

Chapter Eleven

Joseph Turco, Esq., had rented the second floor of a pretty, white two-story building on Main Street, owned by Beth and Peter Mullin, who operated Olde Tyme Floral, a lovely flower shop on the first floor. They were delighted to rent to the young, handsome attorney looking for a place in which to establish a law practice.

I chatted with them in their shop before heading up a short flight of stairs to the second floor. The door to Joe's office was open. He sat behind a desk piled high with law books, and was reading one when I knocked. He glanced up. "Good morning, Jessica," he said, getting up and coming to greet me.

"Hope I'm not intruding on something important."

He said, "Not at all. Just writing a brief to present before the Supreme Court." My face must have reflected I believed him because he laughed and said, "A commercial real estate deal I'm closing on this afternoon. Should have gone smoothly, but one of the parties has thrown a last-minute wrench into the works. Please, come in. Sit down. Coffee is made."

After I'd been served and he'd refilled his cup, he said, "Don't tell me you're having a copyright or plagiarism problem with one of your books."

"Goodness, no. I've been fortunate never to have had a legal problem in my career, and I want it to stay that way."

"Good thinking," he said. "Get us lawyers involved and your problems really get complicated."

"Joe, I'm here on behalf of a friend, Mary Walther."

He frowned, obviously trying to connect with that name. When he did, he said, "Is she related to that farmer, Jake Walther?"

"I would say so. She's Jake's wife."

"Poor woman."

I couldn't help but smile. Even someone who'd been in town only a short period of time was aware of Jake Walther's reputation.

"Sheriff Metzger has arrested Jake and is charging him with the murder of Rory Brent."

Joe's eyes went up, and he whistled softly. "Pretty fast work on the part of our crack sheriff," he said.

"Yes. Mort Metzger is a lot sharper than he sometimes lets on."

"I'm not surprised to hear it."

"What? That Mort is sharper than he—"

"No, no, not surprised Walther's been arrested for murder. To be perfectly honest with you, Jess, Jake Walther is a madman."

Now it was my turn to express surprise.

"Yeah. I had a run-in with him right after arriving in Cabot Cove."

"You did? What led to it?"

"I pulled out of the driveway next to the building one morning. I suppose I should have waited for the pickup truck to pass, but it looked to me like I had plenty of room. At any rate, I pulled into the street and stopped at the light. The pickup truck came flying around on the side of my car and then turned in front of me so that I was blocked. Jake Walther was driving that truck. He leaped out, came to my side of the car, raised his fist at me, and said I was an idiot—I won't repeat all of the words he used because they were pretty foul—and said he'd kill me. I'll never forget the look on his face, Jessica. His eyes were like burning coals, and his mouth was cruel. Yeah, his whole face was that of a crazy person."

"What an upsetting thing to go through," I said. "What happened next?"

"He got back in his truck and drove off. I sat

there shaking when the light turned green. I'd never had anything like that happen to me before."

"How did you know it was Jake?"

"There were two people standing on the corner who witnessed it. They came to the car and asked if I was all right. They told me who he was."

"What an unfortunate experience. Have you had any contact with him since?"

"Are you kidding? Every time I see him in town I make it a point of walking in the other direction. He's nuts, certifiably so."

I decided not to beat around the bush, and simply asked, "Would you be interested in representing him?"

"Represent him? Me? Jake Walther? In a murder case? I've never handled a murder case before."

"I don't think that's as much of a problem as your attitude toward Jake, based on your previous experience with him. You have done criminal law, haven't you?"

"Sure. In New York and New Hampshire, and I've handled a few minor criminal matters since moving here, but nothing heavy duty. Murder? Jake Walther?" His grimace said to me it was out of the question to even consider it.

"I can't say that I blame you," I said. "But Jake's wife, Mary, came to me and asked for help. I thought of you. They don't have any money, and I suppose the state will provide a public defender. But do you know something, Joe? Somehow, I'm not convinced Jake killed Rory Brent."

"Based upon what?"

I shook my head. "I have no idea, and I usually wait until all the facts are in before making a judgment. But it seems that Jake's nasty reputation—and deservedly so, I might add—might be causing too many people to rush to judgment about his guilt."

"Including Sheriff Metzger?"

"Maybe not consciously so, but it's possible. Well, you were good to let me barge in on you in the middle of your work. You look busy, and I'll get out of your hair."

He held up his hand. "No, stay a few minutes, Jess. I'd like to hear more. What do you know about Jake Walther's relationship with Rory Brent?"

I filled him in on what I'd been told, most of it coming from Rory's son, Robert, that there had been bad blood between Rory and Jake, and that they'd had a verbal confrontation during which, again according to Robert Brent, Jake threatened to kill Rory. I also told him about Mary's brother, Dennis, providing an alibi for Jake, but then withdrawing it, and further claiming that Jake had threatened him unless he provided the alibi.

"Interesting," Joe said when I was finished recounting what I knew. "From what you've told me, Sheriff Metzger really doesn't have a lot to hold Jake on."

"Unless there are things I'm not aware of."

"That's always a possibility. But a man not having an alibi isn't reason enough to book him for murder, at least not according to my legal training."

"But what about Dennis's claim that Jake threatened him if he didn't provide the alibi? That would weigh heavily in terms of potential guilt, wouldn't it?"

"Sounds bad, but maybe it isn't. Tell me about this Dennis."

I filled Joe in on Dennis Solten.

"And Sheriff Metzger is depending upon this guy? It sounds like he'd say anything anybody wants him to."

"That's true."

"And Brent's son claiming to have overheard Jake threaten his father really isn't very compelling, either."

"Well, Joe, as I said, there may be other factors at work here that I don't know about."

"You say you've talked to Jake's wife?"

"Yes. I just left her at police headquarters."

"Did you see Jake there?"

"No."

"I hope he didn't give any kind of statement without having a lawyer present."

"I wouldn't know about that."

"The man should have a lawyer with him every step of the way."

"Obviously a good idea. I don't know how fast Legal Aid can get a lawyer here, but—"

"Maybe I'll stroll over to headquarters."

"To talk to Sheriff Metzger?"

"Yeah. And maybe talk to Jake Walther."

"But I thought—"

"No promises, Jessica," he said, standing, taking his suit jacket from where it hung on a wooden coat tree, and slipping it on. "But I wouldn't want to rule it out without having a chance to talk to them."

I, too, stood. "Even though he threatened to kill *you*?"

Joe Turco's grin was infectious. "Maybe Jake Walther had a bad hair day that morning. By the way, what's your interest in this, aside from being friends with Mary Walther?"

I followed him down the stairs. "Nothing other than that, really," I said, not adding that I was thinking of Vaughan Buckley's call asking me to consider doing a true crime book about the Rory Brent murder. Some things were better left unsaid. All I knew was that I'd accomplished what I'd set out to do, and what I'd promised Mary Walther I would do. Whether Joe would follow through was something over which I had no control.

"Mind if I tag along?" I asked when we reached the street.

"I was counting on it. You know, Jess, maybe you should do a book about the Brent murder. One of those true crime books."

"Never crossed my mind," I said.

Chapter Twelve

By the time we walked to police headquarters, Mary Walther had left, telling Mort Metzger she could be reached at home if he needed her. I found it somewhat strange that she hadn't waited for us, considering I'd gone off to fetch an attorney for her husband. Then again, I reasoned, I hadn't given her any assurances that Joe Turco would agree to get involved. It was probably the smart thing to do, to return to the sanctity of her home to await further news.

" 'Morning, Counselor," Mort said when Joe and I entered his office.

"Good morning, Sheriff," Joe replied. "I understand you've made an arrest in the Rory Brent murder."

"Well, now, I wouldn't say I've made an arrest. More a matter of detaining a suspect until the D.A. makes up her mind whether to indict."

"Mind if we sit down?" I asked.

"Be my guest," Mort said, indicating matching wooden armchairs.

"Jessica tells me that you're holding Jake Walther based upon his not having an alibi, and because the deceased's son claims Jake threatened to kill his father."

Mort said nothing, but simply fixed Joe with an expression I'd often seen before, which said that although he was listening, he was not about to be swayed by anything anyone said.

"That really isn't very much to hold a man on, Sheriff," Joe said. "But maybe you know more than we do."

Mort swiveled back and forth in his chair, rubbing his eyes. He eventually stopped the motion, leaned forward, elbows on the desk, and said, "Everybody knows there was bad blood between Jake Walther and Rory Brent. And as far as an alibi is concerned, it's not so much that he doesn't have one. The problem is he threatened somebody if that person didn't give him an alibi."

"You mean Mary Walther's brother, Dennis," Joe said.

"*Ayuh.* When a man feels he needs an alibi that bad, it means he's more than likely done something wrong. At least, that's what my common sense says to me."

"An interesting speculation," said Joe. "But from a legal standpoint, it's hardly sufficient cause to detain a man in jail."

Mort looked at me; I raised my eyebrows to say that I intended to remain neutral during this conversation.

"Mr. Turco," Mort said, "are you here as Jake Walther's legal counsel?"

Now it was Joe who looked at me. I gave him the same eyebrows-up look.

"Probably," was Joe's response. "I'd like to confer with Mr. Walther. I assume he had an attorney present when you spoke with him after . . . as you put it, 'detained' him."

"No need to," said Mort. "I didn't interrogate him, just told him why I was bringin' him in and told him to cool his heels in the cell until this thing gets straightened out."

"Still, Sheriff, there should have been an attorney present from the moment he was in your custody. May I see him?"

"I suppose so," said Mort, standing, going to his door, and yelling for Tom Coleman. A moment later Coleman appeared.

"Take Mr. Turco to see Mr. Walther, Tom."

"Mind if I go with you, Joe?" I asked.

"Sure. Why not? Okay with you, Sheriff?"

"Anything Mrs. F. wants to do is always okay with me."

"That's very sweet, Mort," I said, standing.

Tom led us to the cell in which Jake Walther was confined. I noticed that all the other cells were empty—a slow crime day in Cabot Cove, thank goodness.

Jake was sitting on the narrow, hard cot in a far corner of the cell. He appeared to be sleeping sitting up, and didn't look in our direction when we stopped in front of the door.

"Hey, Jake, wake up," Tom Coleman said, hitting his ring of keys on the bars.

Jake opened one eye and cast it in our direction. He looked horrible. His hair, which was never particularly neat, was a gray, matted mess. Stubble on his face enhanced the look of fatigue and hopelessness. He wore stained bib overalls over a wrinkled yellow shirt. I noted that his shoes had been removed, probably to ensure that he did not attempt to use the laces to harm himself.

"You got company, Jake," Tom said. "Mrs. Fletcher and a lawyer."

Now Jake opened the other eye, turned slightly on the cot so that he faced us, and frowned, saying, "I didn't ask for no lawyer."

"No, you didn't, Jake," I said, "but Mary asked me to find you one. Mr. Turco is new to Cabot Cove, but is an excellent attorney. He's agreed to at least sit down with you. He hasn't committed himself to taking your case, but—"

"Why don't the two of you get the hell out of here," was Jake's reply.

Joe Turco looked at me and shrugged.

I quickly said to Jake, "You can dismiss us if

you wish, Jake, but you should talk to Mr. Turco if only out of respect for your wife. She's very upset, as one can imagine she would be. The least you can do is give Mr. Turco a few minutes so that he can better understand what's going on. Then he can decide whether he would want to represent you. You do need a lawyer, you know."

Jake slowly pushed himself to a standing position, stretched, yawned, and approached the bars. When we were only a few feet apart, he said, "I don't need no damn lawyer. Everybody's already made up their minds that I killed Rory Brent. Might just as well have the sheriff take me out front right now and shoot me, or hang me from a tree. A lawyer? All that'll do is cost money, and he ain't going to be able to do nothing to make it right. Nice you coming here and all, but there's nothing nobody can say to change nobody's mind."

"Suit yourself, Mr. Walther," Joe said. "I'm not crazy about being here anyway. The one time you and I met up before, you cut me off and threatened to kill me."

Jake squinted to better see Joe's face. "That's crazy talk," he said. "I never seen you before in my life."

"Yeah, well, it happened pretty quick. Did you threaten your brother-in-law, Dennis, if he didn't give you an alibi for the morning Rory Brent was murdered?"

Another scowl from Jake Walther. "Hell, no,"

he said. "Dennis has the mind of a mole. Nice enough fella, but he'll say anything anybody wants him to say. Truth is I was out fixing a wall with Dennis when ol' Rory got it. That's what Dennis told the sheriff first time around. But then he changed his mind, probably because the sheriff talked him into it. You can't believe nothin' Dennis says, and that's a fact."

"So maybe we shouldn't believe him when he first said he was with you that morning."

Jake looked at me. "See what I mean, about nobody believing me? This here young lawyer is already trying to tear apart my story."

"I'm not doing anything of the kind, Mr. Walther," Joe said. "I'm just looking at it from the viewpoint of a prosecutor. Did you ever threaten to kill Rory Brent?"

"Might have," said Jake.

Joe turned to Tom Coleman, who stood listening to the conversation. "Mind if we go in the cell with him?" Joe asked. "It's awkward standing out here. And I'd appreciate being alone with—" Joe looked at me and smiled. "With my client."

"I suppose it's okay that you go in," Tom said to Joe, "but I don't think Mrs. Fletcher ought to be in there."

Jake Walther's laugh was a cackle. "What are you afraid of, Coleman, that I'll attack her? Damn fool."

Tom's anger showed on his face, but he didn't respond.

I said, "I'd like to be with Mr. Turco when he talks to Mr. Walther."

"Suit yourself, Mrs. Fletcher," Tom said, unlocking the door and opening it. Jake stepped back to allow us to enter. The moment we were inside, Tom slammed the door shut with unnecessary force, I thought, and walked away, muttering.

"Mind if we sit down?" Joe asked, indicating the cot.

Jake's response was to shrug, go to the other corner, and lean against the wall, arms folded defiantly over his chest.

We sat on the edge of the cot. Joe turned to me and said, "Anything you'd like to ask, Mrs. Fletcher?"

"No, I'm just an interested bystander, here on behalf of Mr. Walther's wife. You're the lawyer. You ask the questions."

"Okay," Joe said. "Let's start from the very beginning, Mr. Walther. Mind if I call you Jake?"

"Suit yourself."

I was impressed with Joe Turco's questioning of Jake. He was forthright, yet gentle, and had a marvelous way of putting Jake at ease, at least to the extent that was possible, considering the circumstances.

"I'm willing to be your attorney, at least for this phase of the case," Joe said a half hour later. "I won't promise anything after that. If you want me to represent you, I'll go straight to the district attorney and demand that she either indict or allow you to go free. But if they let you go, I have to have assurance from you that you won't go any farther than your farm. Understood?"

"What's this going to cost me?" Jake asked.

"We can work that out later," Joe said. "Look, Mr. Walther, I'll be honest with you. I don't like you. The one brush I had with you, whether you remember it or not, was enough to turn me off on Mr. Jake Walther for the rest of my life. I'm here because of Mrs. Fletcher, and because I believe in the law. I don't know whether you killed Rory Brent or not. You say you didn't, and I accept that. I just don't want to see a man falsely accused because of his general reputation. That rubs me the wrong way, as it should rub every citizen the wrong way. Want me as your attorney, Mr. Walther? Speak up now, because I'm leaving."

Jake looked at me, a quizzical expression on his face.

"If I were you, Jake, I'd take Mr. Turco up on his offer," I said. "You have nothing to lose and everything to gain. Again, I remind you that you have a wife who is very worried."

For the first time since entering the cell, I thought of Jake's daughter, Jill, attending school in New York City. "And don't forget Jill," I said.

The mention of her name generated an interesting softening of Jake Walther's face. I wondered whether he might even cry.

"You did a good thing for Jill, getting her into school," he said to me.

Because I knew he'd been adamant in his objection to her attending college, especially one in a big city like New York, I found his expression of gratitude touching.

"I helped her," I said, "because she's a very bright young woman who will make a fine writer one day. Have you spoken with her?"

He averted his eyes as he slowly shook his head and said, "No. She probably don't even know this is happening." He looked up. "But she will."

He turned to Joe Turco. "Sure, go ahead and be my lawyer. How old are you?"

Joe laughed and said, "Thirty-two."

"Too young to be much good at anything, but I suppose you should know somethin' after spendin' all those years in school."

Joe closed the gap between them and extended his hand, which Jake reluctantly took, then quickly dropped.

"I'll be back," Joe said, "I hope with some good news."

I walked with Joe back to his office, where he intended to tidy up a few loose ends on his real estate transaction before seeing the district attorney. We stood on the sidewalk in front of Old Tyme Floral.

"Do you think you'll be successful with the district attorney?" I asked.

"Probably," he said. "They either have to indict or let Jake go. I'm not certain of the Maine statutes, but I'll do some quick reading before I go over there. I'm licensed here, but still have to get up to speed on local law. Think my client is guilty, Jessica?"

"I have no idea, Joe. All I know is that Mary Walther will be extremely grateful for your agreeing to become involved. And I'll see to it that there's money for your fee."

"The last thing on my mind," he said. "Frankly, doing real estate is a lawyer's bread and butter, but it can get pretty dull. Defending the grinch who shot Santa has a lot more pizzazz."

Chapter Thirteen

"O God, whose mercies cannot be numbered; Accept our prayers on behalf of the soul of thy servant departed, and grant him an entrance into the land of light and joy, in the fellowship of thy saints; through Jesus Christ our Lord."

Father Wayne Shuttee, Cabot Cove's Episcopal priest, conducted Rory Brent's burial ritual. The Brent family were staunch Episcopalians; their generosity was well known not only within the church, but throughout the community.

Rory's funeral was held at the town's largest funeral parlor, and had attracted an overflow crowd. Patricia Brent sat stoically throughout the service, which, besides Father Shuttee, consisted of a series of eulogies by townspeople for their departed friend. Bob Brent, the son, wearing jeans with holes at the knees, a T-shirt, and hiking boots, his hair in need of washing, was out of place at such a solemn event. There were muttered comments that he might at least have dressed more appropriately for his father's funeral, but I don't think anyone said it to him directly. Funerals, like weddings, always seem to produce a certain tension within families. The trick is to not feed into it out of deference to the bride and groom, or in this case the departed.

Tears flowed easily as Rory's friends praised him for his civic-mindedness, his exemplary performance as a husband and father, and for what he meant to Cabot Cove. I'd been asked to join the eulogists, but demurred, not because I didn't have good things to say about Rory, but because I knew I would be uncomfortable in that situation. I was content to listen to the words of others, some wonderfully eloquent, others halting and awkward but brimming with honest emotion.

Now, on a dank, dark day, we stood at the gravesite as Rory's coffin was about to be lowered into the hard earth.

". . . ashes to ashes, dust to dust . . ."

"I still can't believe this," Richard Koser, the photographer, whispered into my ear.

"I know," I said.

"It's like . . . well, it's like burying Santa Claus. What will kids all over the world do now?"

Richard's comment caused me to smile. Somehow, there was something comforting about the Santa Claus connection to Rory Brent, even though that link would accompany him to the hereafter.

The coffin was lowered. Father Shuttee said a few final words, and we returned to the cars that had brought us to the cemetery. As I stood chatting with friends, I saw a lonely figure approaching from the far reaches of the graveyard, growing increasingly larger as she neared.

"Isn't that Jill Walther?" someone asked.

"Yes, I think it is," I said.

I wasn't sure whether to close the gap between Jill and myself, or to simply let her reach us. I decided on the former course of action, and took purposeful strides in her direction. My concern was that the speculation that her father had murdered Rory might cause some of those gathered to take it out on her with an unpleasant comment—or worse. Even if Jake had murdered Rory, it was no reason to demonstrate antagonism toward another member of his family.

"Hello, Jill," I said when we were face-to-face on the long, narrow concrete road leading from the main entrance.

"Hello, Mrs. Fletcher."

"How wonderful to see you again. Are you home on your Christmas break?"

"Yes," she said, her eyes focused on her boots. "I left a few days early once I heard about Mr. Brent."

I didn't know how much she knew about the

accusation that her father was the murderer, and didn't want to prompt her. I silently waited for her to say more.

"I came home last night," Jill said. "I guess you know that my father is in jail."

"Yes. I visited him yesterday with an attorney, Mr. Turco. I hope he'll be successful in arranging for your father to be released, perhaps on bail, although when someone is charged with—"

"Charged with murder," she said, completing my sentence. Now she looked me straight in the eye and said, "My daddy could never have killed him."

"I know how you feel," I said, not adding that no matter how much faith she might have, there was still the possibility that the rumors were true, that Jake Walther had, indeed, murdered Rory Brent.

"You don't think he killed him, do you?" she asked. Her eyes were moist, and her lips quivered.

"I certainly don't want to think he did," I said, evading a direct reply to her question. No sense in feeding into her fears at that point.

"Why did you come here today?" I asked.

"I don't know," she said. "I didn't want to stay home. Mom asked me to, but I said I needed a walk. I just headed in this direction. I knew Mr. Brent was being buried and wanted to—" Now she broke down completely, sobs racking her small, slender body. I wrapped my arms around her and pressed her face to my bosom.

"Now, now," I said, hugging her tighter. "I know this is a terrible thing that's happened, but you have to have faith, Jill. If your father didn't do it, he will be cleared in the proper way. Until that happens, you have to be strong. Your mother needs you at her side."

"I know," Jill said, her voice so faint I could barely hear her.

"How is your mother?" I asked.

"Okay, I guess."

Someone called to me that the cars were ready to leave. I waved, then looked at Jill and asked, "Would you like a cup of coffee?"

"Sure. That would be nice."

"Good. There's a new coffee shop not far from here. We can walk there in just a few minutes. Give me a minute to tell my friends I won't be joining them."

When I returned to the vehicles, I was asked whether it was, in fact, Jill Walther. I confirmed that it was. "I sponsored her as a scholarship student at NYU," I said, "and she has some questions for me."

"Amazing how kids can turn out okay even when they have a father like Jake Walther," one of our particularly crusty citizens muttered. I ignored his comment, returned to where Jill stood, and we headed in the direction of The Swan, a delicatessen with a few Formica tables at the rear. It was good to be out of the cold. We were the only people there, and settled in a corner far from the counter. Steaming mugs of coffee in front of us, I smiled and said, "You look wonderful, Jill. New York City must agree with you."

It was evidently the right thing to say. Jill hadn't spoken a word during our walk from the cemetery. But my mention of Manhattan brought a glow to her face and animation to her voice. "I love it there, Mrs. Fletcher. New York City is so alive, so vibrant. It's filled with talented people. I've met so many wonderful writers, and my professors are terrific. I don't think I could ever thank you enough for helping me get the scholarship."

"It was my pleasure, Jill. Just seeing you so enthusiastic is all the thanks I need. Classes going well?"

"Yes. I'm having some trouble with a sociology course, but I'll get through it. I'm getting straight A's in my creative writing courses. And do you know what? I love the history class I'm taking. I hated history in high school. It all seemed so . . . well, so long ago."

I laughed.

"But now I realize that what we are today is based upon what we were back then, so I'm really digging into it. Maybe some day I'll write historical novels."

"One of my favorite types of book," I said. "How did you get home?"

"On the bus. It arrived last night after midnight."

"You must be exhausted."

"No, I'm really not. I guess with what's going on here in Cabot Cove, I won't have time to be exhausted. You said you saw my father yesterday."

"Yes."

"How was he?"

"As well as can be expected, considering he's in a jail cell. Why don't you go see for yourself?"

"Would they let me?"

"I think so. If you'd like, I'll call Sheriff Metzger and arrange it."

Her face turned glum again, and she sat back in her chair.

"Problem?" I asked.

"I'm not sure I want to see him . . . *there*. He might be embarrassed."

"That's always a possibility," I said, "but I'd still suggest you do it. I'm sure he loves you, and he can use love in return at this moment."

"I'll think about it."

"Good. Care for a donut?"

She shook her head. "I'm on a diet."

"Why would you be on a diet?" I asked. "You're a slender young woman."

"But I'm afraid I'll get fat, eating all that rich food in New York. We always ate simple at home. I guess because we never had any money."

"Things have been hard for your family, haven't they?" I said.

I'd learned how financially strapped the Walther family was when I was going through the process of getting Jill the scholarship. Family financial statements had to be submitted, and from what I saw, they lived hand to mouth. Being a poor farmer, of course, has its advantages. There's usually fresh fruit and vegetables in the good weather, and I knew that Mary Walther was an expert canner, which helped them get through the long, harsh Maine winters. But there wasn't any room for luxuries.

"Did you know Mr. Brent very well?" I asked.

My question seemed to sting her. An angry expression came and went on her thin face, and she started to chew her cheek.

"I mean, most people in Cabot Cove knew him, if only as Santa Claus at the annual Christmas festival. I just thought—"

"I didn't know him at all," she said with finality. "Why did you ask that question?" she asked defiantly.

"I'm not really sure," I said. "People say your father and Mr. Brent had a problem. Are you aware of any problem between them?"

"No." The same flat, angry tone.

"I think most of that rumor is coming from Mr. Brent's son, Robert," I said.

If she showed anger before, her face now reflected an inner rage. She took deep breaths, pursed her lips tightly together, and said, "Why would anyone believe anything *he* says?"

"I take it you know Robert Brent."

"Of course I do. We went to school together."

"I didn't mean to make you angry, Jill. It's just that now that I've become involved to some extent with helping your father, I thought you might be able to give me a hint as to the relationship between your dad and Mr. Brent."

"They didn't get along," she said. "I *would* like a donut."

"Of course."

I returned from the counter with two cinnamon donuts on paper plates. Jill took a tiny bite and pushed the plate away.

"Any idea what the trouble was between them?"

She shook her head.

"You know, Jill, when I first met you and started to read what you were writing, I was very impressed by your keen sense of observation. Every good writer is a good observer, or should be, and you demonstrated a remarkable level of it even in high school. It seems to me that your power of observation might have been operating where your father was concerned, especially his relationships with other people, like Rory Brent."

"Mrs. Fletcher, I know you're trying to be helpful, but do you understand how painful this is for me?"

"Of course I do. But the pain will go away if

we can help your father establish his innocence. What was the problem between them?"

She paused, looked up at the ceiling, then back at me, and said, "I don't know."

"And I accept that," I said. "Eat your donut. I'd say it's getting cold, but we both know that isn't the case."

When the plates were empty except for loose cinnamon sugar, I asked, "Want me to make that call to Sheriff Metzger?"

She shook her head and stood. "I really have to get back to Mom. As you said, she needs me. Thanks for the coffee and the conversation. Oh, and the donut, too."

We parted in front of The Swan. As we shook hands, I felt an ache in my heart. Jill Walther was in obvious pain, and I was convinced it had to do with something more than her father having been accused of murder. Something very heavy was weighing on her, and I wanted to know what it was. I felt a certain proprietary interest in Jill Walther, and cared deeply. But I knew I wasn't about to find out much more at that moment, not on a cold December day on a sidewalk in front of a deli.

"I'd like to see you again while you're home," I said.

"You will. I really have to get home now. Thanks again, Mrs. Fletcher—for everything."

"Sure. Take care, Jill. Stop by the house any time."

I considered calling Dimitri Cassis from the deli to get a ride home, but decided against it and set off at a brisk pace. A half hour later, I walked through my front door to the sound of a ringing telephone.

"Hello."

"Jessica? Joe Turco here."

"Hello, Joe. I was at Rory Brent's funeral."

"I was going to go, but decided against it. I really didn't know the man. Besides, I was sort of busy over at the D.A.'s office."

"And?"

"She's not sure she has enough to hold Jake Walther for Brent's murder. I gave her until five this afternoon to make up her mind. Frankly, I think he'll be home for supper."

"That's good news. I think."

"What do you mean, 'I think'? "

"Nothing."

What had prompted my involuntary comment was my ambivalence over whether Jake Walther should be set free. I didn't want to believe he'd murdered Rory Brent. But that didn't mean he hadn't. What if he had committed the murder, was let loose, and ran away, or worse, went on to kill someone else? Wanting something not to be, and having it turn out that way are often two different things.

Turco said, "The D.A. is a nice gal. More willing to listen than some D.A.s I met in New York. If she does let Jake go, she'll set conditions. She might want him to wear an electronic ankle bracelet so his movements can be monitored."

"A small price to pay for being home," I said. "Have you spoken with Jake again?"

"Yeah. I wish I could handle the case without ever having to spend time with him. Damn, he is an ornery type, defying everybody, including me. Must be a joy to live with."

"I'll be here all afternoon, Joe. Will you let me know how it turns out?"

"Of course. By the way, I closed on that real estate deal. Went smoothly."

"That's good to hear. Call me later."

I was immersed in writing Christmas cards when Seth Hazlitt called at four.

"Thought it strange, Jessica, you running off from the cemetery like that."

"Why was it strange? Jill Walther arrived, and I wanted to find out how things were going at NYU."

"*Ayuh*, but it still seemed strange to me. Sure you didn't go off to try and find out more about her father, and whether he killed Rory Brent?"

"Seth," I said, mock indignation in my voice, "I'm a writer in between books who has no interest in crime, real or fiction. I intend to spend the next few weeks simply getting ready for Christmas, and soaking in all the joy of the season. Started your cards yet?"

"Had them written a month ago."

I laughed. Typical Seth, doing things well in advance. Traveling with him always means arriving at the airport hours before a flight.

"Well?" he said.

"Well what?"

"What did you find out about Jake Walther and his relationship with Rory Brent?"

I sighed. "Very little," I said. "I asked, but Jill claims she doesn't know."

"Believe her?"

"Why shouldn't I?"

"How convincing did she sound?"

I thought back to The Swan; not very convincing at all. I told him that.

"I've been doin' some serious thinking this afternoon, Jessica."

"Always good to hear a doctor say that," I said. "Tough case?"

"Haven't been thinkin' about medicine. More a matter of giving some thought to Rory's murder."

"You're infringing on my territory."

"Isn't the first time."

"No, it isn't, and I must admit on those other occasions you were very helpful. Tell me what you've been thinking."

"Not especially keen on doing it over the phone."

"Oh? Something sensitive?"

"*Ayuh*. Thought you might enjoy a quiet supper over here at my place."

"What's on the menu?"

"Not to worry. I don't like Indian food, either."

"Then I'll be there. What time?"

"Make it seven. I'll pick you up."

"No need. Dimitri will do just fine."

I hung up and pondered the conversation I'd just had with my dear friend, the good Dr. Hazlitt.

Too sensitive to discuss on the phone.

That was unusual for him. My curiosity was piqued to such a level that I couldn't concentrate on writing personal messages in the cards, so I put them aside and got busy cleaning the kitchen, my favorite mindless activity.

Dimitri arrived at ten of seven. I was about to leave the house and get in his taxi when the phone rang. I considered letting the answering machine get it, but curiosity got the better of me.

"Hello?"

"Jessica. Joe Turco."

"Hi, Joe. I was hoping to hear from you again. I'm on my way out the door. Has Jake been released?"

"No."

"Oh? A snag?"

"A big one. The county police came up with a footprint in Brent's barn that places Jake there."

"But the sheriff said—"

"Yeah, I know what he said. He didn't find any prints that didn't belong there. He missed one. From what I've been able to gather, the sole print has an unusual mark on it, a break or a tear. Matches perfectly with a pair of boots owned by Mr. Jake Walther."

"Ouch."

"My sentiments exactly. I did my best."

"I know you did. Thank you."

"I still might consider representing him at trial."

"I'm glad to hear that, Joe. I have a taxi waiting. I'll call you in the morning."

"Okay. Funny, but as much as I dislike the guy, I really wanted to make it work."

"And you still may. Thanks for the update. Talk with you tomorrow."

Dimitri deposited me at Seth's house fifteen minutes later.

"How late can I call?" I asked him.

"As late as you want," he replied. "I hired another driver to work at night. His name is Nick. He's a cousin."

"That sounds like a smart move," I said. "Did he just move here?"

"Yes, Mrs. Fletcher. He's living with us. I spent all day showing him where things are in Cabot Cove. You will like him. He is a good driver."

"Just as long as he's as good as you."

Dimitri grinned. "No one is as good as Dimitri. I told him you were my favorite customer."

"That's sweet," I said, patting him on the shoulder from the rear seat. "I'll look forward to meeting your cousin later this evening."

As I stood on the sidewalk and watched Dimitri drive away, a surge of apprehension came over me. I turned and looked at Seth's front door. He'd never before expressed concern about talking to me on the telephone—about anything. What did that mean? I wondered. What startling revelation did I have in store?

The door opened, and Seth's corpulent figure filled the frame. " 'Evenin', Jessica. Come in out of the cold. Scallops wrapped in bacon are just about ready, and the white wine is properly chilled."

Chapter Fourteen

Seth dropped me home a little before eleven. Dinner was good, no surprise. Although my doctor friend wasn't a particularly creative chef, he always did nicely with basic dishes. After scallops wrapped in bacon as an appetizer, we went on to a hearty navy bean soup, followed by what Seth insists is an original recipe—creamed crab meat on freshly baked waffles, a combination I never would have thought of, but admit is delicious—and filling.

But the evening's menu was not foremost in my mind once I was inside my house and had made myself a cup of tea. What did dominate my thoughts, and sent my mind racing, was what Seth had raised over dessert.

Before I could settle in my den and focus upon it, however, I had to return three phone messages that had been left on my answering machine.

The first was from Vaughan Buckley. It sounded

urgent, and he encouraged me to return the call "at any hour."

"Jessica?" he said the minute he picked up the phone.

"Yes. I was out to dinner and just got your message."

"Thanks for getting back to me so soon. I just heard on the news that Mr. Walther has been formally charged with the murder of Santa Claus."

"You mean Rory Brent," I said, not sure why the way Vaughan put it nettled me.

"Yes, Rory Brent."

"Who carried the story?" I asked.

"One of the all-news radio stations here in New York. They're playing it up big, Jess. You know, a brutal murder during the holiday season, a leading citizen of a small Maine town gunned down just weeks before Christmas. On top of that, the victim was that same town's Santa Claus."

I sighed deeply and pulled up a chair. "This is all so unfortunate," I said.

"Yes, it is. Have you given any more thought to doing a book about the killing?"

"I'm really not interested, Vaughan. I'm too close to it, living here and having known both parties."

"You mean Brent and the accused."

"Exactly."

"But that's why you're the ideal person to write a book about it. You know these people, are tuned in to how they think. It's your town, Jess."

"Which is why I wouldn't want to write about something so tragic having happened here."

"We've received calls at the office concerning it."

"From whom?"

"Press. They know you're Cabot Cove's most illustrious citizen. They want to interview you."

"Tell them no."

"I can't tell them that, Jess. They have a right to ask questions, which I assume they'll do starting tomorrow."

"I refuse to be interviewed about this. You know how cooperative I am when it comes to publicity, but this is different."

"Of course it's different, and I'm not suggesting you do this to publicize anything. The publishing industry may have become crass, but not to that extent. I just thought I'd inform you that this little yuletide murder in your beloved town of Cabot Cove has taken on greater significance. It's now a national story."

"Thanks for tipping me off, but as far as doing a book about the murder, I pass."

"Your call, and I wouldn't attempt to influence you. Olga and I are still considering driving up for a few days. Is the offer still good to stay with you?"

"Of course it is. Just give me a day's notice."

The second of three calls on my answering machine was from our mayor, Jim Shevlin.

"Hope I'm not calling too late," I said to his wife, Susan.

"Not at all, Jess. We're watching television, although Lord knows why. All these new cable channels and less to watch. I'll get Jim for you."

"I got your message," I said when he came on the line.

"Good. Have you been getting calls from the press?"

"No, although I just got off the phone with my publisher in New York. He tells me some reporters have called him concerning Rory's murder."

"I've been getting calls, too. There are two TV news crews arriving tomorrow morning, one from Portland, the other from New York.

"TV news crews! I can't believe this."

"I don't want to believe it, Jess. Of course, I suppose the story does have a certain cachet. You know, the Christmas festival, Rory having been synonymous with our Santa Claus, that sort of thing. You've heard, I assume, that the D.A. has formally charged Jake with the murder."

"Yes. Joe Turco called me earlier this evening to give me the news. Something to do with a footprint in Rory's barn."

"Right. It seems the county police picked up a print that Mort missed. It has an odd configuration in the sole, which matches a pair of work boots Jake owns. Pretty compelling piece of evidence."

"I suppose so. What do you suggest concerning the press?"

"We don't have any choice but to cooperate. This story has obviously gone public. Nothing we can do to cover anything up, nor should we. I just thought you might be willing to intercede a little on behalf of the town."

"My publisher said some of them wanted to interview me. I told him I wouldn't agree to be interviewed about something this tragic."

"Which I can certainly understand. But if you were to sort of . . . well, sort of act as the spokesperson for the town, it might take the pressure off me and some other people. We still have a festival to put on."

"Let me think about it," I said.

"Sure. I've called a meeting first thing in the morning to come up with some sort of battle plan. Will you join us?"

"I suppose so. Where and when?"

He told me.

The third call I returned was from Jack Decker, who publishes a monthly Cabot Cove magazine. Jack had been publisher of some of the nation's largest magazines before leaving the hustle-bustle of New York City and settling in Cabot Cove. I had reservations about returning his call. He did, after all, represent the press. But I also knew that he was not someone looking to capitalize on tragedy. His magazine was a loving monthly tribute to the town he'd adopted and had learned to love as much as those who'd lived there all their lives.

"Was hoping you'd get back to me tonight," he said.

"I assume you're calling about Jake Walther being formally charged with Rory Brent's murder."

"Exactly. I spoke with Jim Shevlin earlier this evening. He's concerned that the story has been picked up by the national media, and that some of them are heading for Cabot Cove tomorrow. I suggested he tap you as the official spokesperson for the town."

"That was *your* idea. Thanks a bunch, Jack."

He laughed. "Makes sense. Any reporter who shows up here will want to talk to you anyway, considering your stature. You might be able to deflect their attention."

"That's a role I'm not anxious to take on. I told Jim I'd attend a meeting with him tomorrow morning."

"I'll be there. We can discuss it then. By the way, I understand you were the one who got Joe Turco as Jake Walther's attorney."

"Word does get around. Yes. I brought Joe into the situation. He's not particularly fond of Jake Walther—but then again there aren't many Jake Walther fans around, are there? But he agreed to take the case, at least in its preliminary stages. Looks pretty bad for Jake, doesn't it?"

"I'd say so. Well, see you in the morning."

"Yes, you will. Best to Marilou."

All calls returned—and hoping no one else

would call that night—I sipped my tea, which by this time had become cold, and seriously pondered what Seth Hazlitt had told me at dinner a few hours before.

What he'd related to me was shocking in and of itself. Compounding it was the difficulty he'd had in deciding to share it with me. He was appropriately circumspect, which I understood, considering the sanctity of the doctor-patient relationship. But that consideration was mitigated by the importance of the information as it related to Rory Brent's murder, and Jake Walther having been charged with it. Poor Seth, I thought. He'd found himself between the proverbial rock and a hard place. That he chose to share the information with me was, at once, flattering, yet unnerving. But now that he had, I had an obligation to follow through, whether I wanted to or not.

The problem was that I wasn't sure how to proceed, whether to have another discussion with Seth, or simply to act upon what he'd told me.

An hour later, without having come to a definitive conclusion, I decided that what was most needed was a good night's sleep. Tomorrow was another day, as the saying goes, although that contemplation wasn't especially pleasant, considering what it might hold in store.

Chapter Fifteen

The meeting started out in Mayor Shevlin's office, but quickly shifted to the courtroom because of the number of people who'd decided to attend.

Cabot Cove's courtroom doesn't get much use. It's in session two nights a week to handle traffic violations and other minor infractions, but seldom hosts anything resembling a prolonged trial. The last one I could remember was a year ago when Sheriff Metzger, working in concert with state police, broke a car theft ring operating out of an auto repair service on the outskirts of town. Stolen cars from all over the state were brought to this repair place to be painted, and to have their VINs altered. The trial lasted six days; the accused were convicted and sent to a penitentiary in northern Maine.

"Well, looks like we have a media event on our hands," the mayor said once he'd gotten everyone to settle down.

"A media circus, you mean," one citizen replied. "It's a disgrace to be known as the town where Santa Claus was murdered."

"I second that," someone else said.

"It doesn't matter what any of us feel," Shevlin said. "The fact is a murder did take place in Cabot Cove, and the victim happened to be the person playing Santa Claus at our yearly festival. Obviously, that has piqued the interest of folks in the media, and they're coming here to report the story. Now, it seems to me that what we have to accomplish here this morning is to come up with a way to manage things so that everything goes smoothly, and that Cabot Cove comes off in the best possible light."

"I have something to say," Seth Hazlitt said. He and I sat next to each other in the front row.

"Yes, Dr. Hazlitt?"

"Rory Brent's murder doesn't have anything to do with the average citizen of this town. You know how reporters are. They'll be pokin' their noses into everybody's backyard, trying to get some dumb answer from them on how they feel about the murder. If you want to protect the image of Cabot Cove, I suggest anybody arrives here from the media be herded up and kept on a short leash. The story they're interested in is the murder. We've got a victim, and we've got the accused. The only access these folks from out of town should have is with Mort and his people, the D.A., and anyone else involved in the legal aspects of the case. After that, they shouldn't be allowed to talk to anybody."

A few people applauded.

Priscilla Hoye, chairperson of the Christmas festival, stood and faced the crowd. "I would be the last one to debate anything with Dr. Hazlitt," she said. Priscilla is an attractive middle-aged woman with short blond hair and a sunny disposition. She'd forged a successful career in public relations in the travel industry, but, like attorney Joe Turco, had become tired of the hectic pace of life in Manhattan, gave up her New York office, and moved to Cabot Cove. Her natural marketing and public relations skills had been quickly put to use by the festival committee.

She continued. "But I think we might be missing an important point. Yes, we don't want this unfortunate situation to cast a pall over the festival. At the same time, as you all know, we've pursued wider coverage of the festival than just Maine media outlets. We were delighted when that network talk show decided to broadcast from here last year during the festival. We send out news releases to all the major national media. So, having them arrive, even though it's for a different purpose, should be put to good use. An integral part of the story is that this murder occurred during the weeks leading up to the festival, and that this town refuses to be set back by it. The festival is going forward, and it promises to be the most successful in its history. I'm sure we can maneuver the press in such a way that they'll balance their reports of the murder with upbeat, positive stories about the festival and the town."

Now Seth stood. "Can't say that I agree with you, Priscilla. Seems a little naive to think the press would do anything positive. All they want is stories about blood and gore."

Priscilla, who'd remained standing, said, "I know that's the popular perception of the media, Seth, but it isn't necessarily accurate. I've been dealing with the press for many years, and I can assure you that if handled right, Rory Brent's murder will be only a part of the story, not the whole story."

"Seems like we should listen to Priscilla," a citizen said. "She's the expert when it comes to these matters."

"Nope, I go with the doc," said a gentleman from the rear. "Reporters are a bunch 'a ghouls. Let's do like Doc suggests, herd them up and make sure they don't stray."

A spirited discussion ensued, with those in attendance pretty much split on whose side of the argument they favored. As usual, our diplomatic mayor settled the matter by suggesting a committee be formed to make a decision about how much latitude to give reporters. Seth declined to be on the committee, and I was asked if I would participate. It wasn't high on my priority list, but I accepted.

"All I can say is you'd better get this committee workin' pretty fast," Seth said disgustedly. "From what I hear, the vultures will be descending on us any minute."

With that, the door to the courtroom opened, and two young men and a young woman entered. The men carried portable video equipment, including lights and a microphone dangling from a long boom. The young woman, obviously the reporter, led them up the center aisle and to the front of the courtroom.

Mayor Shevlin looked down from where he sat at the judge's bench and asked, "Who might you be?"

"Roberta Brannason, Fox News."

Shevlin straightened his tie and buttoned his suit jacket. "Welcome to Cabot Cove," he said in a voice usually heard only when he was campaigning.

"Thank you," Ms. Brannason said. "Who runs things around here?"

"Pardon?" Shevlin said.

"Who's in charge? We're here to cover the Santa Claus murder."

Shevlin looked to where Seth Hazlitt and I sat. He frowned, pursed his lips, then turned to the reporter and said, "I'm the mayor of Cabot Cove.

But I suppose you'd like to speak with our sheriff, Morton Metzger."

The lights held by one of the two young men came to life, and the cameraman, the videocamera propped on his shoulder, began recording.

"I'd like to speak with a lot of people," Ms. Brannason said, "starting with the person in charge of your Christmas festival."

"That would be Ms. Hoye," Shevlin said, indicating Priscilla, who went to the TV crew and introduced herself.

"We'd like to interview Jessica Fletcher, too," Brannason said.

"She's sitting right over there," Priscilla said, pointing at me.

The reporter, followed by her two colleagues, came to where I sat with Seth. "Roberta Brannason," she said, extending her hand. Seth and I stood; I shook her hand.

"I'm glad you're in town, Mrs. Fletcher," said Brannason. "I understand you travel a lot."

"Usually I do, but this Christmas I'm staying close to home."

"I understand you might be doing a book about the murder."

"I'm afraid you've received faulty information."

Ms. Brannason turned to her crew and said, "Let's get a wide shot of this room and the people in it," then turned to Shevlin. "Is this meeting about the festival and the murder?"

"Well, yes and no. Actually, we knew you were coming and—"

Brannason ignored him and instructed her crew where to position themselves.

She turned again to me and asked, "After we get some wide shots, I'd like to go where I could interview you in private, Mrs. Fletcher."

"I'm afraid I'm not about to become an interview subject, at least not where this tragic incident is concerned."

By now, with the meeting thoroughly disrupted, people had gathered around us.

"You probably know more about the case, Jessica, than anyone else, except for the sheriff and the district attorney," a woman said.

"Oh, no, you're wrong."

"Is the sheriff here?" Brannason asked.

"No," Seth Hazlitt said. "Got better things to do than hang around waiting for somebody with a camera and a microphone."

Ms. Brannason ignored him and asked me again if I would consent to an interview. Before I could answer, Jack Decker, the magazine publisher, who'd joined our little knot of people, said, "I think that's a splendid idea."

I glared at him.

"Jack may be right," Seth chimed in.

The reporter waited for the crew to join her.

"You'll have to excuse me," I said, overtly checking my watch. "I have an appointment."

"What's your phone number?" the reporter asked.

"It's . . . I'm in the book. Excuse me."

Seth followed me to the courtroom door. "Where are you runnin' off to in such a hurry?"

"I have an appointment with . . . with Dr. Colarusso."

"You just had your teeth cleaned."

"I know, but I feel a sudden toothache about to come on."

He looked at me quizzically, but didn't say anything else. I left the courtroom, walked briskly down the hall to the front door of town hall, and stepped outside. The sky was deep blue and without a cloud, the sunshine bright and glistening off the snow. I walked a block to a public phone, stepped inside the booth, pulled a scrap of paper from my pocket on which I'd written a number, and dialed it. A man answered.

"This is Jessica Fletcher. I'm calling from Cabot Cove. Dr. Seth Hazlitt called you on my behalf."

"That's right, he did," the man said gruffly.

"I'd like very much to talk to you . . . today, if at all possible."

There was a long silence.

"What time would be convenient for you?" I asked.

"I'm not sure we should be having this talk, Mrs. Fletcher."

"I know how delicate the topic is, Mr. Skaggs,

but as you know, someone's life may hang in the balance."

After another prolonged silence, he said, "Noon? At my office?"

"That would be fine. Can you give me directions?"

After he had, I hung up and stepped out into the lovely December day. My temptation was to call Skaggs back and cancel our appointment. But I knew I couldn't do that, now that I'd put things into motion. I had no idea where the visit would lead, but if it would shed any light on what had happened to Rory Brent, I owed it to him, to his family, to Jake and Mary Walther—and to myself—to pursue it.

Chapter Sixteen

Thomas Skaggs lived in the town of Salem, about forty-five minutes south of Cabot Cove, just over the county line. I considered asking Dimitri to drive me there, but decided that discretion was the better part of valor in this situation. I checked the bus schedule and caught the eleven o'clock, which made a stop in Salem on its way to New York City.

I hadn't traveled on a bus in years, and found the experience enjoyable, although I suppose I might not have had the same reaction were I taking a longer trip. The ride was smooth and without incident; forty minutes later, I got off in front of Salem's small town hall.

I stopped someone on the street and asked for directions to the address given me by Skaggs. This friendly citizen gave me a big smile and informed me it was only two blocks away. I thanked her and walked slowly in the direction she'd indicated.

Minutes later, I was in front of a prewar, two-story brick building in what appeared to be a residential area. I looked around; it was the only commercial building within sight.

I approached and read names on small brass plates affixed to the right side of the door. There were six occupants of the building, all of them having something to do—at least according to their names—with social work or counseling. The name at the top of the row was Here-to-Help, the organization run by Mr. Skaggs.

I stepped inside and looked at a directory on the wall. Here-to-Help was upstairs in office number six. I climbed the stairs, went to the door with the organization's name on it, and knocked. A woman's voice said, "Come in."

I stepped into a cramped reception area, where a middle-aged woman with carefully coifed silver hair sat behind a metal desk.

"Yes?" she asked.

"I'm Jessica Fletcher. I have a noon appointment with Mr. Skaggs."

"Oh, yes, we've been expecting you. I can't tell you what a pleasure this is, Mrs. Fletcher, to actually meet you in person. I've read most of your books—Mr. and Mrs. Skaggs have, too—and we love them. Imagine, you living so close and never having met you. This is an honor." She got up, came around the desk, and extended her hand. "Let me tell Mr. Skaggs you're here."

"Before you do that, I'm a little unsure of what Here-to-Help does."

"Oh, I think Mr. Skaggs would be the best person to explain that to you. But basically, we're a resource for young men and women who've made a wrong turn in life and need some sort of restructuring."

"You mean counseling?"

"Yes, we do a great deal of that, too. But primarily we point them in the direction of other agencies that can more directly help them, depending upon the problem they bring to us."

The door opened, and we both turned. Standing in the doorway was a mountain of a man with a black beard, ruddy cheeks, and glasses tethered to his neck. He wore a rumpled tan safari jacket over a blue denim shirt, jeans, and sneakers.

"Jessica Fletcher?"

"Yes. You must be Mr. Skaggs."

"Tom Skaggs, and I would appreciate it if you would call me Tom."

"Provided you call me Jessica."

"We're already off on the right foot," he said in a deep, gravelly voice. "Please, come in."

His office wasn't much bigger than the reception area, but it had a comfortable feel to it because of the dozens of framed autographed photographs on the walls. I glanced at a few, which were pictures of him with familiar political faces.

"My personal rogues' gallery," he said. "You don't get paid a lot in this business, but you do meet a lot of important and self-important people. I keep telling the bank that holds the mortgage on my house that these pictures are worth something, but they never seem to agree."

I laughed. "I suspect there are millions of people with that same problem, doing important good work, but not being recognized for it by bankers."

"Well said. Please, sit down."

I took one of six director's chairs that formed a semicircle to one side of his desk. He plopped into a large, high-backed leather swivel chair and propped one sneaker—it had to be size fourteen—on the edge of the desk. "Well," he said, "I have a feeling you're about to cause me to break one of my most stringent rules."

"Which is?"

"Never to discuss anyone who's ever stepped through this door."

"I can understand and appreciate that, Tom, but I'm sure you agree that the circumstances make it the perfect time for you to break that rule."

"You may be right. From what I've been told by Seth Hazlitt, this could represent one of those extenuating circumstances. I believe in the law, but sometimes it has to be broken if the cause is great enough. Same goes for bureaucratic rules. Fill me in. Seth did his usual shorthand explanation. I suspect that you, being the great writer you are, will do a better job of weaving the tale."

"I'm not sure being a writer will help me in this situation, but I'll try to be concise. I'm a great believer in the old adage, 'If I had more time, I would have written less.' "

His laugh was as big as his body. "I like that," he said. "Go ahead. I'm all ears."

"I'm sure you've heard about the murder of Rory Brent, a successful farmer in Cabot Cove, and a man loved by everyone in town."

"Santa Claus at your yearly festival."

"Exactly. Our sheriff has made an arrest in the case, a gentleman—another farmer—named Jake Walther."

"Yes, I've heard about that, too."

"Jake Walther is disliked by many people," I said. "He's an unpleasant sort of man, rough-hewn and without what might be termed a warm and fuzzy personality. He was immediately suspected of the murder, mostly because of having rubbed people the wrong way. The deceased's son, Robert, claims that Jake Walther threatened his father, said he was going to 'blow his brains out.' "

"Sounds like the motive was there."

"Oh, yes, if the son is to be believed. At first, our sheriff only *questioned* Jake Walther in connection with the murder. Jake claimed to have had an alibi provided by his wife's brother, Dennis, who lives with them on the farm. But then

Dennis changed his story and said he'd been threatened by Jake if he *didn't* provided that alibi. I should mention that Dennis is somewhat impaired. He's the sort of person who will agree with anything in order to not offend. There's speculation that our sheriff might have pressured him into changing his story, although I tend to dismiss that theory, knowing our sheriff as I do."

"I'm sure you're right in that assessment, Jessica, although it's possible, isn't it, that your sheriff influenced this fellow, Dennis, without meaning to."

I nodded. "Yes, that is always a possibility. I brought a young lawyer into the case, and he was confident Jake Walther would be released, based upon the grounds the sheriff and district attorney were using to hold him—nothing more than the deceased's son's claim that there was bad blood between the two men, and that Dennis had changed his story and says Jake threatened him. But then the county police discovered a footprint in the barn where Mr. Brent was murdered, and they further claim that Jake Walther owns a pair of work boots with a unique characteristic in the sole, some sort of tear or rip that matches the print found in the barn. Based upon that, he's being formally charged with the murder."

I sat back, confident I'd accurately portrayed the situation.

Tom Skaggs, too, leaned back and ran his hand

over his beard. Finally, he came forward in his chair, placed his elbows on the desk, and cradled his chin in his hands. "I take it you aren't convinced that this Jake Walther committed the murder."

I shook my head. "No, that's not quite right. I don't know whether Jake Walther killed Rory Brent or not. Based upon this new piece of evidence involving the boot, I have to go with the sheriff's decision to charge him with the crime. On the other hand, there was such an obvious rush to judgment that I must wonder whether even our sheriff, and the district attorney, have been unduly influenced by public condemnation of Jake Walther. I'm not trying to clear him of anything. But I'm also determined that an innocent man not be charged with a heinous crime. We have the Christmas festival coming up, and you know how important that is not only to us in Cabot Cove, but to thousands of others who've come to depend upon our festival as an affirmation of the Christmas spirit."

Skaggs pondered what I'd said, stood, then went to a gray metal, four-drawer file cabinet in a corner of the office, where he withdrew a folder. He returned to his desk and opened the file.

"I understand how sensitive this is, Tom. But I also hope you see the necessity of knowing what actually happened. It could have an important bearing upon this case."

His response was to nod and flip through pages in the file, asking as he did, "Are you involved in this, Jessica, because of a professional interest? As a writer of crime novels?"

"Goodness, no," I said. "My publisher did ask me to consider writing a nonfiction book about the case, but I've declined. On the other hand—"

He glanced up. "On the other hand?"

I smiled. "On the other hand, I must admit to a certain genetic curiosity that has held me in good stead when writing my novels, but that sometimes gets me in trouble."

He returned my smile. "Curiosity killing the cat?"

"Fortunately, not yet. I just want to make you aware that I'm cognizant of the difficult position this puts you in, just as it put Dr. Hazlitt in an awkward posture."

"No need to further explain. If I wasn't going to open these files to you, I would have said so right from the beginning. I've known Seth Hazlitt for years. He's one of the most honorable and ethical physicians I've ever met, and I come in contact with a lot of them because of what we do here. No, I'm willing to share this with you and answer your questions, provided we keep it between us, in this room. In other words, you can use what you learn, but can't tell anyone where you learned it. Fair enough?"

"It will have to be."

"Okay, here's what happened. Jill Walther was referred to this agency by Dr. Hazlitt a year ago. She was a senior in high school, and I understand was a very good student. I'm also led to believe that she was not the sort of young woman who might be termed 'promiscuous.'"

"I certainly would concur with that. I got to know Jill pretty well because of her writing talent. I arranged for a scholarship for her to New York University."

"I didn't realize that. A nice thing you did for her."

"I did only what I thought was justified."

"Does Jill know everything going on with her father regarding the murder?"

"Yes. She came home on Christmas break a few days early once she heard about it. She's with her mother at the farm."

"You say you got close to her. She never mentioned any of this?"

I shook my head. "Not a word."

"I suppose I'm not surprised," he said. "The reason she was sent here, after all, was to get her out of your county. I was reluctant when Seth Hazlitt first called about her. My experience has been that when a young person messes up, it's better to face things right where they are, with the people they know. But there seemed to be some additional pressure involved, and I certainly wasn't about to say no. We seldom do when a young person is referred to us."

"I know that Dr. Hazlitt referred her to you," I said. "I also know the reason she went to him."

"A sad thing when a high school girl becomes pregnant. It's a national epidemic. For some reason, these young women think having a baby will give their lives something worthwhile, something to love and to love them back. They never stop to realize that they've put their entire lives on hold, never consider the tremendous financial responsibility having a child entails."

"I certainly agree with that," I said. "Tragic when a young woman forfeits her future by becoming pregnant before she's ready emotionally and financially to raise a child in the proper way. But my understanding from Seth Hazlitt is that this was not the result of a deliberate act on her part. There was the question of whether she was raped, and became pregnant by virtue of that."

"That's right. Frankly, I honestly don't know the circumstances that led to her pregnancy. She told me she'd been raped, but it wouldn't be the first time I've heard that from a girl suffering guilt, and trying to lay the blame off on something, or someone else. Did Dr. Hazlitt indicate what he felt had actually happened?"

"No. He told me she claimed when she went to him that she'd been raped. She wanted him to arrange for an abortion, even do it himself. Of course, he refused and urged her to go to the police. She said she couldn't do that."

"Exactly the same thing she told me when she was here. Does Dr. Hazlitt have any idea who the alleged rapist was?"

"Not that he told me. Did she give a name to you?"

He shook his large, shaggy head. "I urged her to bring charges, too, but she was adamant about not doing it. I have the feeling she was afraid that if she named the person, there might be serious repercussions. I didn't press; it's not my job to press."

I thought for a moment, then asked, "Did she come here seeking an abortion?"

"Yes."

"And you refused as well, I assume."

"We're not in the abortion business. I wanted her to stay in our group home for a few days and receive some counseling before making up her mind about what to do. She refused that as well. I gave her the names of two respected abortion clinics. That's protocol with Here-to-Help. I pointed out other options—delivering and keeping the child, or putting it up for adoption. All I could do."

"Did she come here alone, Tom? I mean, was she accompanied by anyone?"

"Not that I'm aware of. I asked her whether someone had brought her, and she said no. I felt very sad seeing her walk out of this office after the brief conversation we had. She seemed like an extremely intelligent and decent girl. I think I could have helped her if she'd stayed."

"Do you know if she went on to get an abortion?" I asked. "I mean, I suppose I have to assume she did since I'm not aware she had a child. If she did have a child—no, that's impossible. I spent a great deal of time with her throughout her senior year. She must have aborted the baby."

"I'd say your assessment is correct."

"Do you have any idea *where* she had the procedure performed?"

"Not a clue."

"Did she pay for your services?"

"No, nor was she asked to. We're funded by the state, some federal funds, and charitable donations. We don't take money from the young people we serve, although there are times when a family member will insist upon making a donation to the agency. We never turn them down." He laughed.

"Did anyone offer such a contribution on her behalf?"

He grunted as he searched for an answer. "Not that I can recall, although sometimes such contributions are made long after the young person has been helped by us, and made anonymously."

"Do you keep records of contributions made according to their source? I mean, would you have a list of contributors to this agency from, say, Cabot Cove?"

"Mrs. Witherspoon is a fanatical record keeper. She makes a note of everything. I wouldn't be surprised if she has the height and weight of every contributor in her files, along with eye and hair color. Want me to ask her?"

"If you would."

He left the office, leaving me with some time to consider what he'd said. That Jill Walther had become pregnant in her senior year of high school was certainly a shock, not because I'm unaware that such things happen, but that it happened to her. Of course, her claim that she'd been raped cast a very different light on her situation—if that claim was true.

I was still digesting what he'd told me when he poked his head in the door and asked, "How far back do you want me to go?"

"Not too far," I replied. "Maybe the period immediately following her visit to you."

When he returned, he carried with him a computer printout. He sat behind his desk and scrutinized it while I waited. "Yeah, there were a couple of donations from Cabot Cove during the three months following the date of my meeting with Jill. A couple of small contributions, but one impressively large." He laughed again. "We could use more people like this. Interesting donor, based upon what you've told me."

"May I see the list?"

"Sure."

He positioned the printout on his desk so I could peruse it. The name came off the page with physical force. Rory Brent had made a contribution of five thousand dollars shortly after Jill Walther sought the counsel of Here-to-Help.

Chapter Seventeen

I had to wait two hours for a bus back to Cabot Cove, and spent the time browsing quaint shops and enjoying a tuna salad sandwich in a pub that seemed to be a popular gathering spot for Salem's business community.

I was virtually alone on the bus, for which I was grateful. I've always found traveling, whether on a plane, an ocean liner, or even a bus, to be good thinking time. The problem was the bus ride was so short that I'd barely began to codify what I'd learned from Tom Skaggs when we pulled up to the small, two-bay bus station in Cabot Cove.

It was four-thirty. Although the sun continued to shine, albeit with less intensity as it neared the horizon, the weather had turned colder, the sort of bone-chilling, dry cold that seems to occur only on clear winter days in Maine.

Dimitri's cousin, Nick, was parked at the curb. I got in the back of his taxi and he drove me home.

"How are things working out?" I asked as I signed the small chit that would become part of my monthly bill for cab services.

"Very good, ma'am," he said. "I like it here. This is a good place."

"Cabot Cove? Yes, it certainly is," I said, getting out of the taxi as he stood holding open the door. I'd reset the timers on my outdoor lights to go on earlier, and the one in front did as we stood in my driveway, illuminating the pretty wreath on my door.

"Are you getting ready for Christmas?" I asked.

"Oh, yes, but there is so much to do. America is a busy place, especially when a holiday comes."

"It certainly is," I said. "Thank you for the ride. Say hello to Dimitri."

I brought in the mail, turned up the heat, which my frugal New England heritage has me turning down to the lowest possible level whenever I'm not there, and made a fire in the fireplace.

I sat at the kitchen table and started going through my mail. Most of it consisted of bills, although there was an envelope with only my handwritten name on it. I opened it and read:

Mrs. Fletcher—I want very much to interview you about the Santa Claus murder. I'll make myself available any hour of the day or night—you name the time and place. Other people in town have been very cooperative all day, and I was hoping to meet up with you again. We're staying at Morton's Boardinghouse—it was the only place we could find rooms in town. Please call me the minute you get this message—Roberta Brannason.

She included Morton's phone number.

I put the note aside; I was in no mood to talk to Ms. Brannason, or any other member of the press for that matter.

The phone rang.

"Hello?"

"Jessica. Seth here."

"Hello, Seth. I just came back from Salem."

"Yes, I know. Tom Skaggs called. You'll have to fill me in on what transpired between you."

"Well, he basically confirmed that—"

"Not on the phone, Jessica. Free for dinner?"

"Yes, although I'd prefer to have a quiet dinner alone right here at the house."

"As you wish. Heard from the reporters?"

"Only Ms. Brannason, the reporter from Fox News. I take it more have arrived."

"*Ayuh,* they certainly have. You'd think the president of the United States was holdin' a summit meeting in Cabot Cove. Got to hand it to Priscilla Hoye. She seems to have them all pretty much in hand. Knows how to deal with them, somethin' I wouldn't want to do."

I laughed. "They can be an aggressive lot, that's for certain."

"By the way, Jessica, seems to me we ought to start pickin' the stories we'll be readin' to the children at the festival."

"You're right, although I thought we should confer with Cynthia before making any decisions."

"My thinking exactly. Well, if I can't get you to agree to let me buy you dinner, I'll wish you a good evening."

"And the same to you, Seth. Please understand. I'd love to, but not tonight."

"Of course. But I do think we should hook up tomorrow, say at my office at ten? I don't have patients till one."

"Fine. Put me in your appointment book."

Although I wanted to settle down for the evening, content myself with some snacks for dinner, and get back to writing Christmas cards and answering correspondence, I was too restless to accomplish any of that. I found myself pacing the house, the events of the past few days flooding my brain. So I did what I often do when faced with such mental confusion. I took out a yellow legal pad and pen, sat at my desk, and listed everything I'd learned to date:

> The victim, Rory Brent, successful farmer and beloved figure in town, found murdered in his barn a half mile from his house wearing only shirtsleeves. Killed sometime in the morning.

> Brent's wife, Patricia, away visiting her

cousin, Jane, in Salem, Maine. (Just occurs to me that Tom Skaggs and his Here-to-Help organization is located there, too.)

> Patricia says she took an early bus, the trip took forty minutes, and she returned on the one o'clock bus.

> Brent's son, Robert, seemingly untouched by his father's death—claims Jake Walther threatened his father. Known that bad blood existed between Rory Brent and Jake Walther. Walther disliked by many people in town.

> Walther initially claims his brother-in-law, Dennis, was fixing a stone wall with him the morning of Brent's murder. Dennis confirmed that. Then, Dennis changes his story and says Jake threatened him unless he provided that alibi, and that he was *not* with Jake the morning of the murder. Question is, can Dennis be trusted in what he says?

> Jake's wife, Mary, seeks help for her husband. I bring attorney Joseph Turco into picture. Looked like Jake would be released until county police determine that a footprint on the barn's dirt floor, missed by Mort Metzger, had a unique sole print matching boots owned by Walther. Walther now charged with Brent's murder.

> Jill Walther, Jake and Mary's daughter, pregnant in senior year—referred to a social agency in Salem by Seth Hazlitt. Tom Skaggs confirms that a pregnant Jill Walther came to him, and that he gave her names of two abortion clinics. Also says he counseled her on other options, in-

cluding giving birth and keeping the baby, or putting it up for adoption.

> Jill Walther claimed she was raped, but refuses to name the person. Who was it?

> Shortly after Jill's visit to Here-to-Help, Rory Brent makes a big financial contribution. What connection does the Brent family have with Jill's pregnancy?

> My next move? Confront Jill Walther with my knowledge she'd become pregnant? To what end? I have no right knowing that information—unless it bears directly upon murder, it should remain her business. Still, could be a valuable piece of information. Possibility: discuss it with Mort Metzger. No!!!! If I do anything, must be face-to-face with Jill.

I'd no sooner written that last line when the phone rang. It was Roberta Brannason, the Fox News reporter.

"Glad I caught you, Mrs. Fletcher," she said brightly.

I wish I could say the same.

Instead, I said, "Well, you have. I was gone for the day."

"Mind if I ask where?"

My guffaw was involuntary. "Of course I mind. Where I go is none of your concern."

"I just thought it might have to do with the Santa Claus murder."

"Ms. Brannason, Santa Claus was not murdered

in Cabot Cove. Mr. Rory Brent was, a leading citizen. Frankly, I think treading upon the fact that he played Santa Claus at our yearly festival is distasteful."

"Hey, Mrs. Fletcher, don't jump on me. I'm just developing a story the way my bosses want me to."

"Well, maybe you should tell your bosses they're on the wrong track. Now, what can I do for you?"

"Give me a half-hour interview."

"Out of the question. I told you I would not grant an interview having to do with this tragedy."

"I talked to your publicity director at Buckley House in New York. She said she hopes you'll cooperate. Help sell books, you know."

I am normally a very patient person, and I understand the need of reporters to press as hard as they can to get a story. After all, that is their job, and I respect it. But there are times when the press has strained my patient nature, and this was developing into one of those times.

I tried to divert her attention by saying, "I understand a number of your media colleagues have arrived."

"Yes. It's a big human interest story, Mrs. Fletcher. I understand how you feel, but the public has an insatiable appetite for stories like this, especially when they involve a major holiday—like Christmas."

"That may be, but—"

"Were you in Salem today following up on some aspect of the murder?"

"Was I in—? How did you know I went to Salem?"

"By asking a few simple questions around town. My network has sent up two investigative reporters to help me develop the story. Someone at the bus station said you'd bought a ticket to Salem."

"I must say, I'm impressed, Ms. Brannason."

She laughed. "We're pretty good at what we do. Isn't Salem where Mr. Brent's wife went the morning he was murdered?"

"I'm even more impressed now."

Another laugh. Then, in a more serious tone, "Look, Mrs. Fletcher, I don't want to unduly interfere with your life. But we're going to do this story one way or the other, and it really would mean a great deal to have the famous Jessica Fletcher, the most illustrious citizen of Cabot Cove, give me an on-air interview. Please? Won't you at least consider it?"

"I'm always willing to consider most anything, Ms. Brannason."

"Call me Roberta."

"I'll think about it . . . Roberta. In the meantime, I'm busy this evening doing some paperwork. I'm sure I'll see you around town tomorrow. We can chat then." I didn't give her a chance to respond because I quickly added, "Good night. Thank you for calling," before hanging up.

I received other calls that night before going to bed, none of them having to do with the murder. Mostly they were from people wanting to discuss the upcoming festival. I enjoyed those conversations. They certainly were less weighty than murder.

But the final call of the evening, which came in just as I was preparing to go to bed, was from Joe Turco.

"Hope I'm not calling too late," he said.

"Not at all. I'm happy to hear from you. Anything new?"

"I'd say so. They're releasing Jake Walther."

"What? Why? How did that come about? I thought—"

"It seems there's some conflicting theories about that footprint found in Rory Brent's barn. The county police say it matches the sole on one of Jake's boots. But another scientist from the same lab claims they don't match. Anyway, while they're thrashing out conflicting theories, I put the arm on the D.A. I've been with her all night. I told her that she absolutely has nothing to justify holding Jake in jail. As I told you, she's a pretty levelheaded person. She finally agreed with me that there wasn't enough evidence to indict, and so he's being let go. Should be on his way back to the farm by now."

I had the same ambivalent set of feelings as when it was first anticipated that Jake would be allowed to go free. I was delighted for him and his family. On the other hand, I had that lingering question of what would happen if he had, in fact, killed Rory Brent.

But I couldn't let that color my thinking. The man was innocent until proved guilty, and up until this point no such proof existed.

"You've done a marvelous job for someone who dislikes his client so much," I said.

His laugh was weary. "Every lawyer I know has done work for clients they couldn't stomach, absolutely hated. It isn't important how a lawyer feels about a client. What *is* important is that the law be followed, and justice be served. I'm just glad it worked out this way, at least for his wife and daughter. I just learned about her. Jill, is it?"

"Yes. She and I . . . well, Joe, it was good of you to call and give me the news. You sound like you could use some sleep."

"What I could use is a drink and some dinner," he said, "which I intend to take care of right now. Good night, Jessica. Talk to you tomorrow."

Before going to bed, I added a final item to my list:

Jake Walther released. What next?

Chapter Eighteen

"Hello, Mary."

I'd just finished showering when Mary Walther called.

"No, you didn't wake me. I've been up for an hour. I heard the good news about Jake. Joe Turco called me last night to tell me he'd arranged for Jake's release."

Mary Walther's voice did not mirror the sort of joy I expected. She said flatly, "I suppose it's good news, Jessica, although I have to be honest with you. I'm very worried."

"About Jake?"

I thought back to my previous conversation with her in which she'd indicated her concern that Jake was capable of doing something destructive. It was that conversation that had led Seth, Mort, and me to the farm, resulting in Mort's taking Jake into custody. Was she voicing the same concern this time?

I asked.

"I don't know how to explain it, Jessica," she said. "Naturally, I'm pleased that he's not in jail any longer. But—"

"But what?"

"Could you come to the farm today? I know it's an imposition—I've imposed upon you enough already—it is, after all, the Christmas season, and I know how busy you are, but I just thought—"

"Of course I'll come. How is Jill doing?"

"That's part of my concern. You will come?" Her voice brightened.

"Yes. What would be a good time for you?"

"Well, I'm not quite sure at the moment. Maybe midday? Yes, about noon. I'll make some lunch."

"No need to do that," I said. I knew of their dire financial situation; the last thing Mary Walther needed, with everything else on her plate, was to be making lunch for visitors.

"I look forward to you coming," she said.

I dressed, tidied up the house, and checked my personal calendar for the day. I'd promised to meet with Seth Hazlitt in his office at ten. Other then that—and, of course, with a trip to the Walther farm now on the schedule—I was relatively free, which meant I might actually get around to doing some Christmas shopping.

In previous years, when I'd been away from Cabot Cove in the days leading up to Christmas, I'd done my shopping in big cities like New York or London. Shopping for gifts in Cabot Cove would be a welcome deviation from that pattern, and I looked forward to it. With only a few exceptions, Cabot Cove's shopkeepers are extremely pleasant and helpful. Not only do they offer an array of interesting and useful gifts, there is psychic satisfaction from buying locally and supporting their efforts.

It was an overcast day, but no snow in the forecast, and I decided to walk into town. I'd put on my down jacket, hiking boots, red-and-black plaid scarf, and woolly hat, and was about to go out the door when the phone rang. Rather than pick it up, I let the answering machine do its work, and stood next to it waiting to hear who was calling. Call screening certainly comes in handy on occasion.

I wasn't surprised that it was the Fox news reporter, Roberta Brannason. "Please, Mrs. Fletcher, just fifteen minutes for an interview. I promise I won't take any longer than that. I'm not sure where we'll be during the day, but if you're in town, I'm sure we'll bump into each other."

Glad that I'd opted to not pick up, I set off at a brisk pace toward the village. I had a few minutes to kill before my ten o'clock appointment with Seth, and stopped in to visit with Peter and Beth Mullin in their flower shop. With Christmas coming up fast, Beth and seasonal helpers she'd hired for the holidays were extremely busy. Her husband, she told me, was spending most of his time making deliveries—"Cuts into his poetry writing," she said, laughing. When Peter wasn't helping run the shop, he was writing poetry for which he'd gained a sizable reputation in Cabot Cove, and gave Monday night poetry readings at a trendy, cozy coffee house that had opened within the past year.

"Anything new on Rory Brent's murder, Jess?" Beth asked, not looking up from an elaborate floral arrangement she was creating.

"No," I said, "except that Jake Walther has been freed."

That announcement stopped her in midtask. She looked at me, eyes opened wide, and said, "I hadn't heard that. I thought they'd pretty much identified him as the murderer."

"That's the prevailing understanding of most people in town, Beth, but there's evidently been a classic rush-to-judgment. Something to do with a conflict over the lab analysis of the shoe print found in Rory's barn. Jake is back at the farm."

Beth frowned and bit her lip. "I'm not sure letting Jake Walther loose was a great idea."

"Why do you say that?"

"Oh, we all know the man is irrational. And irrational people can do . . . well, irrational things."

I had to silently agree, although I worked hard at the moment to override my emotional response with a more cognitive one. I decided not to respond, but asked instead, "Is Joe Turco upstairs?"

"I think so," she said, returning to her arrangement. "He came in a few minutes before you did."

"Think I'll pop up and say hello," I said. "Save some poinsettias for me, Beth. I love them in the house this time of year."

Joe Turco was drinking coffee and munching on Danish when I arrived at his open office door.

"Come on in," he said.

"Just stopped by to say hello, and to thank you for letting me know about Jake's release."

"I suppose I should consider it a legal victory."

I entered the office and took a chair across the desk from him. "Why do you say you 'suppose' you should consider it a legal victory. It is, isn't it? I mean, from a lawyer's perspective, arranging for a client to be released has to be viewed as some sort of triumph."

"I know, I know," he said, wiping his mouth with a paper napkin and tossing it along with the empty Styrofoam cup and paper plate into a wastebasket. "Maybe if the guy were a little nicer, I'd feel better about it. When I went down to police headquarters to give him the news and escort him out, all he did was glare at me and growl some obscenity. He's a real head-case, Jess. What's that word for it? You know, that Maine slang."

"*Jo-jeezly*," I said. "I really feel bad having gotten you involved with him."

"Don't. I did what I was supposed to do as his attorney."

"What will happen now? I mean, what's the next legal step?"

"That depends on whether the labs get their story straight on the shoe print. The D.A. released Jake on his own recognizance. He's been told he can't leave the farm. There was some talk of using an electronic monitoring system, something strapped around his ankle that can be monitored from a central station."

Thinking of the concern Beth had expressed downstairs, I said, "That sounds like a sensible idea. Why wasn't it done?"

"Because Sheriff Metzger and his department don't have such a system. He could have gotten it from the county, I suppose, but the D.A. decided not to press it. Walther assured her he would abide by the rule to stay at his farm, and he promised me the same thing—when he wasn't cursing under his breath."

"I got a call from Jake's wife. She sounded concerned now that Jake is back home, and asked me to come to the farm to talk with her. I'm going there at noon."

"Well, give my best to my lovely client if you see him. In the meantime, I have to get a contract ready for a closing this afternoon. This business with Jake Walther cut into my normal routine, put me behind a little."

"Did Jake say anything about paying you?" I asked.

"No, of course not, and I wasn't looking for it. There's nothing else for me to do at this point. Unless, and until, the D.A. can resolve the dispute between the lab people and come up with more of a solid case against Jake, he'll cool his heels at his farm. I could petition the court to force the D.A. to officially remove him as a suspect, and to have the home restriction lifted. But I have to think about that a little bit. I'm not sure it's the right move to make at this juncture. Good to see you, Jess. Have a good day."

Seth Hazlitt had just finished frying up a batch of apple fritters when I arrived, and insisted I join him for one, and coffee, at his kitchen table.

"Anything new, Jessica?" he asked.

"No. Oh, did you hear that Jake Walther has been released?"

"*Ayuh,*" he said, pouring maple syrup over his fritters. "Spoke with Mort first thing this mornin'. Seems the lab folks have a bit of a conflict over Jake's boot."

"That's what I was told. Enough of Jake Walther. Let's get down to choosing stories for this year's reading. By the way, the fritter is excellent."

Seth showed me a list of Christmas stories he'd jotted down on a yellow legal pad. "I especially like this one," he said, pointing to the title, " 'The Dog That Talked at Christmas.' "

"I don't think I'm familiar with it," I said.

"Lovely story. About a dog that breaks the canine code of silence. You know, all dogs can talk, but they know that if they do, they'll have to go to work."

"Who wrote it?"

"Wonderful writer named Laurie Wilson."

"Fun," I said, laughing. "What are the other stories you'd like to do?"

"Got a couple of others, Jessica. Not as well known as the standard ones. Ever hear of 'A Christmas to Remember,' by a fella named Coco?"

"Can't say that I have."

"Nice story. Santa comes to help a brother and sister fix a broken star on their Christmas tree."

"And does he?"

"And does he *what*?"

"Fix the star."

"Of course he does. He's Santa Claus."

"A happy ending. Good. That's two. I was thinking of 'Carl's Christmas.' "

"Doesn't ring a bell."

"By a wonderful writer named Alexandra Day. It's about a dog named Carl who—"

" 'Nother dog story."

"They're always the best. Carl is put in charge of a family's baby and takes the child on a Christmas tour of everything wonderful about the season. Beautifully illustrated, too."

"Speaking of illustrations, I got Cynthia to agree to blow up pictures from the books we use, maybe even project 'em on a screen."

"That's a wonderful idea. What's next?"

We eventually decided on five stories—"Nutcracker Ballet," the Christmas staple "Rudolph the Red-Nosed Reindeer," "The Dog That Talked at Christmas," "The Lonely Snowman," and "The Littlest Christmas Elf."

By the time we finished, it was almost eleven-thirty.

"Well, this was a fruitful session," I said, "but I have to run. I'm due at the Walther farm in a half hour."

Seth fixed me in a quizzical stare. "Didn't know you were goin' out there, Jessica. What brings this on?"

"I forgot to mention it. Mary called and asked that I speak with her."

"Strange," Seth said.

"Why?"

"Now that Jake is back home, I wouldn't think there'd be any reason for you to go out to see Mary. Did she say what she wanted to talk about?"

"Just that she was worried. I suppose she needs a female shoulder to lean on. Even though Jake has been let go, this still must be a terribly stressful time for her. For all of them."

"I suppose it would be. Sure you don't want to think twice about it, Jessica?"

I stood, put on my coat and hat, and went to the front door. "I don't see any reason why I shouldn't go out there, Seth. I feel sorry for Mary and want to be as much help as possible, especially at this time of year. To be facing these sorts of troubles at what should be a joyous season makes it doubly difficult."

"Why don't you stop by here on your way back home. I'd like to hear what transpired."

"If I have time. Will you call Cynthia with the list of stories?"

"*Ayuh*. Do it the minute you're gone. How are you gettin' there?"

My laugh was involuntary. "I forgot to call Dimitri," I said. "Silly of me. Can I use your phone?"

"No need. I'll drive you."

"I wouldn't put you out like that."

"No trouble at all."

"But I don't know how long I'll be there. I don't think you should come in with me."

"I won't wait—just drive you there and drop you off. You can call Dimitri for a ride back."

"All right," I said. "But we'd better get going. I don't like to be late—to anything."

* * *

We drove slowly to the Walther farm, taking in the scenery as the village slowly melted into countryside. Seth was deep in thought; I eventually asked him what he was thinking.

"I was thinking how unsettling this whole Rory Brent business is. I mean, everybody points a finger at Jake Walther. He's questioned by Mort, then arrested. They're going to let him go, but then they discover a footprint in Rory's barn that matches one of Jake's work boots. The D.A. decides that's enough evidence to charge him with the murder. But then the lab experts can't agree whether the footprint really matches the boot, so they let Jake go. I suppose what I'm wishin', Jessica, is that it would be resolved one way or the other—right now! Either Jake Walther killed Rory Brent and is officially charged with the crime, or he's absolved of any guilt. This town needs some closure." He turned and looked at me. "You agree?"

I nodded. He was right. With the Christmas festival getting closer and closer, not having a resolution to Rory's murder made things that much worse. Which is not to say that I would want Jake Walther falsely accused in order to neaten things up. But if Rory Brent's murderer had been identified beyond a reasonable doubt, it would go a long way to putting to rest the minds of a lot of people in Cabot Cove.

Seth was the first to spot the vehicles parked

on the road in front of the Walther farm. There was a television remote truck with a huge antenna protruding through its roof, and three cars. People milled about.

"Damn press," Seth said, slowing down.

"Not unexpected," I said. "Everyone knows that Jake Walther has been released and is confined to the farm. That's where the action is, at least as far as the media is concerned."

Seth pulled to the side of the road and stopped, then started to make a U-turn.

"What are you doing?" I asked.

"Heading back to town. You don't want to be in the middle of this media feeding frenzy."

I put my hand on his arm. "No, I'm going in to see Mary Walther. I promised, Seth. I suspect she needs me, and I want to be there for her."

His sigh said many things, mostly that he was frustrated with me. Nothing new there.

"Drop me in front of the farm," I said, "and go back into town. Take care of whatever it is you have on your agenda. They can't make me talk to them, and I won't. I'll simply go into Mary's house and spend some time with her. Okay?"

"You are a stubborn woman, Jessica Fletcher,'" Seth said, turning the wheel and proceeding toward the other vehicles.

"I know," I said. "But you're still my friend, aren't you?"

Seth chuckled. "Can't imagine anything you

could do to change that," he said. "If you have trouble gettin' hold of Dimitri, give me a call and I'll come back out to get you."

"Fair enough."

When I opened the door to get out of Seth's car, those standing in front of the farm immediately headed in my direction, led by the Fox TV reporter, Roberta Brannason.

"Mrs. Fleltcher, good to see you. Did you get my message?"

I lied. "No. Did you call me?"

"Yes. I got your answering machine. But it doesn't matter because here you are."

"Yes, here I am," I said.

"Did you come to see Jake Walther?" she asked.

"I'm here to see his wife, Mary. Excuse me. I have an appointment with her."

I started to walk up the narrow, rutted road leading past the first house on the property, in which Jake lived, and to the middle house, where Mary—and, now that she was home from college—where Jill Walther lived, too. I glanced at Jake's house as I passed. There was no sign of life. The curtains were closed. So was the door. Then I noticed smoke wafting from a metal chimney pipe jutting up through the roof. Someone was there, presumably Jake.

Ms. Brannason and members of her crew fell in step behind me.

I stopped halfway up, turned, and said, "Please.

Mary Walther is a friend of mine, and I'm here on a social visit. I have nothing to say to you, so I suggest you go back to your vehicles and continue waiting for something to happen. It's not going to happen with me, I assure you."

I started to resume my walk when Ms. Brannason grabbed my arm. Her action angered me; I turned and glared at her.

"Mrs. Fletcher, all I'm trying to do is my job. I don't want to intrude on your life. I know that you're a famous personality, and I respect that. But I don't understand why you won't talk to me for even just a few minutes. You probably know more about what's going on with Mr. Walther and the investigation than anybody else in town, except maybe for the sheriff and the district attorney. What are you *hiding*?"

"Hiding? I'm not hiding anything. But if I were, it is my right to do so. I understand that you are doing your job, and I'm not looking to hinder that. But it doesn't mean that I'm under any obligation, legally, ethically, or morally, to talk to you about this tragedy that has occurred in a place I love very much. Maybe later today, or tomorrow. In the meantime, I'm running late for a date with a friend. Have a good day, Ms. Brannason."

I stepped up onto the porch of the house, hesitated, then knocked on the door. I heard sounds from inside. Eventually, the door opened, and the frame was filled by Mary Walther.

"Hello, Mary."

"Thank you for coming, Mrs. Fletcher," she said, holding open the door.

"I'll come in only if you call me Jessica, or Jess."

"I know, you've said that before. I'm sorry. Please come in . . . Jessica."

I stepped into the small, spartan living room. I didn't immediately notice that another person was present, sitting in a wooden chair in a corner to my right. I turned and looked. It was Dennis Solten, Mary's brother.

Dennis hopped to his feet and lowered his head so that his eyes were directed at my feet. He held a crumpled hat in his hands and wore soiled bib overalls and heavy boots.

"Hello, Dennis," I said.

He managed to glance at me past the top of his head, nodded, muttered something unintelligible, and returned his focus to the floor.

"I hope you don't mind that Dennis is here, Jessica," Mary said. "I thought you might be interested in something he has to say."

"I'm always happy to see Dennis," I said. "I remember the good work you did around my house, Dennis. As a matter of fact, there are some things I could use help with now."

"Yes, ma'am," he mumbled.

"Please, let me take your coat," said Mary, reaching out. I slipped out of my coat and handed it to her. As she went to another corner of the room to hang it on pegs protruding from the wall, I took the moment to glance about the room. Although it wasn't particularly attractive, there was a certain warmth and comfort to it that was appealing.

"Please, sit down," I said to Dennis. He did as he was told.

"I made some tuna salad and tea," said Mary.

"I'm really not very hungry, but if it's made, I'd love some. Tuna is one of my favorites."

"It's with real mayonnaise I make myself," said Mary. "I know I should offer some with low fat—everybody seems to be eating low-fat things these days—but I've just never gotten into that."

"Sometimes I think people are into it a little too much," I said. "Homemade mayonnaise will be just fine."

Mary went to the kitchen, leaving me alone in the room with Dennis. It was obvious he was not about to initiate conversation, so I took the lead.

"How have you been, Dennis?"

"Pretty good, I guess," he replied, not looking at me.

"I suppose you were very busy when Jake was away from the farm."

"Yes, ma'am."

"You must be happy to have him home again."

"Yes, ma'am, only . . ."

I sat forward in my chair. "Only what?"

"Jake, he's . . . he's sort 'a mad at me."

"Is he? What is he mad about?"

"About what I said to the sheriff."

"Yes, I know what you mean. The problem was that there was confusion about what you said. First you claimed you were working with him the morning of Mr. Brent's murder, but then you said something else. And if I'm not mistaken, you said Jake threatened you if you didn't tell that original story."

Dennis didn't answer, just slumped a little more in his chair and nervously twisted the brim of his hat. It was then I realized that he and I were not completely alone. I turned; Mary stood in the kitchen, peering into the living room.

"Dennis and I were just chatting about Jake's being home," I said to her.

She seemed surprised that I'd noticed she was listening, and said, "That's nice. Would you like tea, or I have some raspberry lemonade."

"Tea would be fine."

"I'll only be a minute," she said, disappearing from my view.

Dennis and I sat silently until I said, "Mary said you might have something interesting to tell me, Dennis."

He squirmed in his chair and tightened his grip on the hat.

"Dennis? What was it you wanted to say?"

I glanced over my shoulder; Mary had positioned herself again so she could observe and listen.

Dennis drew a series of deep breaths, rolled his eyes around looking at everything but me, then said into the air, "I wasn't with Jake that morning."

"That's what you told Sheriff Metzger the second time. Did Jake really threaten you if you didn't originally claim that you were with him?"

I don't know what he said, but it seemed to indicate an affirmation.

"Why are you repeating this to me now?"

" 'Cause . . . 'cause Mary will tell you I'm not lyin'."

I turned once again in the direction of the kitchen, but Mary wasn't there this time.

I returned to Dennis. "What do you mean that Mary will tell me you aren't lying?"

" 'Cause she knows where I was that morning. She was with me."

I sat up straight and processed what he'd said. Why hadn't Mary come forth before with information that would prove that Dennis had not been with her husband the morning of the murder?

I turned in my chair and looked up at Mary, who now stood directly behind my chair. "Dennis says that—"

"It's true, Jessica. Dennis wasn't with Jake that morning."

"Where was he?"

"Helping me tend to the chickens."

"The chickens? Here on the farm?"

"Yes."

"Why didn't you tell Sheriff Metzger this right away?" I asked.

"Because I didn't want to hurt Jake. It was better that the sheriff think Dennis was with him."

"But that's . . . that's withholding evidence, Mary. It amounts to lying to the sheriff."

"I did it because Jake is my husband. A wife should stand by her husband."

"I certainly agree with that, in most instances. But Jake was charged with murder. Whether he had an alibi was crucial for the authorities to determine who killed Rory Brent."

"I suppose you're pretty disgusted with me, Jessica."

"Not at all. I can understand the dilemma you were in. It must have been a very difficult decision to make."

"I'm a God-fearing woman, Jessica. Always have been. I was taught not to lie, and I never do. But when they said Jake had killed Rory Brent, I just knew I had to help him."

I turned to Dennis. "And you told the sheriff you were with Jake because Jake threatened you if you didn't?"

"Yes, ma'am."

"What caused you to change your story?" I asked.

"I dunno. I guess I just didn't like having to lie to the sheriff. Made me nervous. I get nervous a lot."

I understood, but didn't see the need to reinforce his sudden pang of conscience.

I turned to Mary. "Why are you telling *me*? Have you told anyone else?"

"No."

"Will you? Will you go to the sheriff and tell him this?"

"I don't want to, that's for certain."

"If you don't want the sheriff to know, why not just keep it entirely to yourself?"

Her broad face became a mass of wrinkles as she pondered the answer. Finally, she said, "Because like I said before, Jessica, I'm a God-fearing woman. I feel like I did when this thing first happened, when I had to make a decision about what to tell people. I don't know what to do, and that's the plain and simple truth. You were the one I came to right away when Mr. Brent was killed, and when Jake was acting strange. I came to you because you seem to have a level head on your shoulders, and would help me do the right thing. I feel that way now, and that's why I asked you to come here today. What should I do, Jessica?"

"I'm afraid I have only one answer, Mary, and that's for you to go to Sheriff Metzger and tell him this. No one can make you do that, but it's the right thing. It's the *only* thing, especially for someone who, as you say, fears God."

The truth was, I'd never been someone who believed in fearing any God. For me, God—whoever he or she might be—is a benevolent force somewhere out there, to be loved, never feared. But I understood that there are many people who were brought up to believe different, and this was not the time to get into a religious debate.

"Will you go with me to the sheriff?" Mary asked.

"No, Mary. This doesn't directly concern me. I suggest you call him. If you want to do that while I'm here, that's fine. But no, I don't think it would be appropriate for me to go with you."

"But you came over with that young lawyer to help me. You were at the house the night the sheriff took Jake away. It would mean a lot to me, Jessica, to have you at my side when I go in and admit my lie, admit that I did a terrible thing."

I stood and placed my hands on her beefy arms, looked her in the eye, and said, "Mary, you haven't done a terrible thing. You've been under tremendous stress, and I'm sure the sheriff will understand that."

Her face became soft, almost childlike, and I wondered if she was about to cry.

"Yes, I'll come with you to the sheriff."

We didn't bother eating lunch that day. Ten minutes after Mary had made her confession, we

were outside and ready to climb into their bat-
tered pick-up truck. The press was still camped
on the road.

Dennis got behind the wheel. I was about to
get in the truck when I remembered that Mary
had said on the phone she was worried about Jill,
whom I'd forgotten about.

"Where is Jill?" I asked.

"Sleeping."

"In your house?"

"Yes. Poor girl. She's been crying her eyes out
ever since this happened."

I turned and looked at the small house. An upstairs curtain parted, revealing Jill Walther. Although I was a distance from the window, I could
see the anguish etched into her pretty, young face.
I raised my hand to wave, but she quickly closed
the curtain and was gone from my sight.

"I'd like to see Jill again before she goes back
to school," I said.

"I don't think that will be possible," said Mary.

"Why?"

"I've convinced her to go back early—day after
tomorrow."

"She won't be home for Christmas?"

"Better to be away from here until all this is
settled," Mary said.

"I . . . well, that's your decision . . . and hers."

As we slowly drove down the rutted access road,
we had to pass the house in which Jake lived. He

was on his small porch. I thought Dennis might stop, but we drove right past without acknowledgment. I looked in the rearview mirror and saw him clearly. He was leaning against the door and holding a rifle that dangled at his side. It was a chilling sight, one I would not soon forget.

Roberta Brannason and the other members of the press stood on the road. She waved; I didn't return it. What I was thinking was that I hoped she, and her colleagues, wouldn't be foolish enough to approach Jake. He looked like he meant business.

Chapter Nineteen

I accompanied Mary Walther and Dennis into police headquarters, where Sheriff Mort Metzger sat in his office, eating a slice of pizza. He glanced up, wiped his mouth with the back of his hand, and came around the desk. "What brings you here?" he asked.

"Mary has something to tell you, Mort," I answered.

"Oh?" Mort's eyebrows went up. "And what might that be?"

"Maybe we ought to sit down," I suggested.

"Sure, Mrs. F., sure thing."

Since there were only two spare chairs in his office, he yelled out the door for someone to bring in a third.

Once seated, I looked at Mary, gave her a smile of encouragement, and said, "Go ahead, Mary. It's the right thing to do."

Mary told Mort that she'd been with Dennis the morning of Rory Brent's murder.

"Doin' what?" Mort asked.

"Tending to the chickens and trying to fix a wall of the chicken coop that was falling down," she said.

Mort looked at Dennis. "That true, Dennis?"

Dennis nodded, hat clenched tightly in his hands, eyes focused on the floor.

"So, what you're saying," said Mort, "is that not only was your original story about being with Jake that morning a lie, you now have someone to corroborate your second story, that you *weren't* with him."

"Yes, sir," Dennis mumbled.

"Okay," said Mort. "But what about your claim, Dennis, that Jake threatened to hurt you if you didn't come up with that first story about being with him? You still stand by that?"

Dennis glanced nervously at Mary before replying, "Yes, sir. He certainly did."

Mort sat back in his chair, formed a tent with his hands beneath his chin and grunted. After a moment, he said, "I appreciate your coming in to tell me this. But I've got to tell you, Mary Walther, that lying to a law enforcement officer isn't taken lightly around here."

I said, "But she didn't lie, Mort. She simply didn't offer the information, and I don't think you asked her whether she was with Dennis that morning."

"Maybe lying is too strong a term," Mort said.

"But it certainly involves withholding information. Wouldn't you agree, Mrs. F.?"

I didn't answer. It seemed to me there was no longer a reason for me to be there. I said, "Mary confided this in me, and we agreed to come to you, Mort. She wanted to get it off her chest because it was weighing heavy. I admire her for that."

I gave her another smile.

"Now that she has," I said, "and unless you have anything else to ask her, I suggest we all get about our business."

"No need for you to stay, Mrs. F.," Mort said. He turned to Mary and Dennis. "But I'd like you two to hang around a few minutes more. I've got a couple of questions that need answering."

A look of panic came over Mary's face. I stood, went to where she sat, placed my hand on her shoulder, and said, "There's nothing to worry about. All you have to do is tell the truth."

Mort said, "You realize, don't you, Mrs. Walther, that what you've told me this morning isn't calculated to help your husband any."

Mary agreed.

"I suppose you didn't want to tell me this in order to protect him."

"Yes, sir, that is the truth," she said. "A woman has to stand by her man. That's the way I was raised."

"Admirable enough, but sometimes when the law is involved—especially murder—that rule doesn't always hold up."

"I'll be off," I said, "I have things to do."

"Want a ride back home?" Mort asked. "Tom can—"

"No, thank you, Mort. I have errands to run here in town. Besides, a walk will do me good. Good-bye, Mary. Good-bye, Dennis."

Mary stood and thanked me for my support. Dennis didn't move from his chair, although a slight twitch of his head indicated, I suppose, that he was responding to my words.

I walked at a leisurely pace from police headquarters to the center of town. My first stop was the Post Office, where I'd heard they were selling a special edition of Christmas stamps. I bought a hundred of them on self-stick sheets, spent a few minutes chatting with Debbie and Jim, two of our friendly, helpful postal clerks, left the building, and stood on the street. It was still overcast, and a breeze had picked up from the east. Although snow hadn't been forecast, I could smell it in the air. You live in Maine long enough and your nose becomes extremely sensitive to the possibility of snow, no matter what the official forecast.

I went to the building housing Olde Tyme Floral, waved to Beth, and went up the stairs to Joe Turco's office. He didn't see me in the doorway because he was hunched over an office machine in the corner of the room. I cleared my throat. He stopped what he was doing, turned, and shook his head.

"What are you doing?" I asked.

"Trying to program phone numbers into this new fax machine I just got. Ordered it from a catalogue. Great machine, but it takes a Ph.D. in space science to program in the numbers. You've got to push one button after another, and by the time I remember to push the next one, the menu the previous button brought up is gone."

I laughed. "How are you at programming VCRs?"

"Even worse than programming fax machines."

"Well, don't let me interrupt you."

"I'm glad you did. What's up?"

We sat, and I filled him in on what had happened that morning with Mary Walther and Dennis.

His response was to shake his head and say, "Not good for my client."

"I suppose not, although the fact that Dennis can't provide an alibi still doesn't say Jake murdered anybody."

"True, but it just keeps looking worse and worse for him. Maybe the lab techs will never get together on the shoe print. That's the key piece of evidence. If they ever come to an agreement, Jake will find himself facing a jury."

"Joe, I was wondering if you would do me a favor."

"If I can."

"I'm interested in what the town records indicate about the Walther farm."

"What do you mean?"

"Well, Rory Brent's son, Robert, claims that his father and Jake Walther had a real falling out. I remember distinctly his saying that they argued more than a month ago over 'land and money.' Yes, those are precisely the words he used. 'Land and money.' "

"So?"

"So, I've been around long enough to have seen some pretty irrational behavior where land and money are involved. What I'm wondering is why such an argument would take place between Jake and Rory Brent. Rory's farm isn't adjacent to Jake's property. What interest would Rory Brent have in the Walther farm?"

Turco chewed his cheek, shrugged, ran his index finger around the inside of his ear, and said, "I can't imagine public records would shed any light on that, Jessica, but I'm willing to take a look. Easy to do."

"I know it is, and I realize I could do it myself. But I just thought that any information contained in those records might have more meaning for an attorney."

"Could be. I'll hop over to Town Hall right now if you'd like."

"No rush. You do have that new fax machine to program."

"No, I don't. I think I'll give it up and just punch in numbers when I need to send a fax. Or, have a couple of stiff drinks later today before trying again. Where will you be for the rest of the day?"

"In town. I promised Seth Hazlitt I'd drop by his office after coming back from the Walther farm. I'll do that, get in a little Christmas shopping, and then head home."

"If I come up with anything, I'll give you a call." I started to leave the office, but he stopped me. "You know what I've been wondering lately, Jessica?"

"What's that?"

"I've been wondering where Rory Brent got his money."

"Oh? That seems fairly obvious. He ran an efficient and profitable farm. At least that's what I've always heard."

"I've heard that, too. But I have some successful farmers as clients. While they do pretty well, none of them will ever get rich working the land."

"I suppose not. It's a tough way to make a living, as the saying goes. Maybe Rory had family money. Or Patricia."

"Maybe. Just a thought. I'll be in touch."

Seth was with a patient when I arrived at his office, located in a wing of his stately Victorian home. His nurse, Pat Hitchcock, who worked part-time for him, greeted me warmly and said he wouldn't be long.

"Any other patients due?" I asked.

"No. Slow day, Jess. Getting ready for Christmas?"

"Trying to. I thought I'd block out this afternoon for some shopping."

"My shopping was done a month ago," Pat said. "All my cards written, too."

"I envy you. Every year I promise myself to get a running start on cards, have them in the mail no later than the middle of November. But as my father used to say, 'The road to Hell is paved with good intentions.' "

"How true, how true," she said. "Excuse me, Jess. I have to get some paperwork done before I leave."

Seth's patient, a young woman named Anne Harris, who'd recently moved to Cabot Cove, was introduced to me by the good doctor.

"I've wanted to meet you since moving here," she said. "I do some writing of my own."

"Really? What sort of writing?"

"Nothing major. Some poetry, short stories."

"Short stories," I said, "the hardest form of writing."

"So I've heard. I thought I'd like to try my hand at writing a murder mystery."

"Then you should do it," I said.

Seth, recognizing a familiar scenario in my life—someone aspiring to write murder mysteries and wanting me to become involved—said, "Good to see you Mrs. Harris. You pick up that prescription and take it until it's run out, heah?"

"I promise," she said lightly.

When she was gone, I followed Seth to his

study, where he was engaged in—what else?—the writing of last-minute Christmas cards. He poured tea from a teapot Pat Hitchcock had placed on his desk and said, "All right, fill me in, Jessica. What happened out at the Walther farm?"

I told him.

"Must have been difficult for Mary to tell that to Mort. Doesn't do her husband's case any good."

"Yes, it was difficult for her, Seth, but I'm proud that she found the courage to do it. I also stopped in Joe Turco's office before coming here."

"And how is our young attorney friend?"

"Just fine, although he's having trouble programming phone numbers into his new fax machine."

Seth laughed. "You'd think they'd come up with a way to make programming those infernal machines easier. Must be some sort of plot against consumers. Time for Ralph Nader to get involved."

"Seth, Mary told me Jill Walther is going back to college early, leaving the day after tomorrow."

"That's odd, isn't it?" he said.

"I thought so. I asked her about it, and she said she thought it was better for Jill not to be here in Cabot Cove while all of this is going on with her father. I've got to talk to her before she goes."

"Shouldn't be difficult. Just go back out there."

I shook my head. "No, Seth, there was something in Mary's tone that told me *she* did not want me to talk to Jill. She didn't state that, of course, but I sensed it."

"Why would she want to keep you from speaking with her daughter? After all, Jessica, you were the one who got her into college, got her that scholarship. Seems to me you'd be the first person welcome at the house."

"I feel that way, although what I did for Jill doesn't give me any automatic rights to spend time with her. But I have to see her, Seth. I have to clear up, if only for my own sake, this business of Jill's having sought abortion counseling, and Rory Brent's making a big contribution to the counseling center right after she was there. I'm also intrigued with what Robert Brent said."

"Which was?"

"Robert said his father had argued with Jake Walther over 'land and money.' That's why I stopped up to see Joe Turco. I asked him to check public land records to see if there was any link between Jake Walther and Rory Brent from a real estate point of view. I just know there's a relationship of some sort between those two men that goes beyond Jake's surly disposition."

"*Ayuh*, you may be right, Jessica. Funny, while I was waiting for Mrs. Harris to arrive, I started thinking about Patricia Brent."

"Rory's wife?"

"*Ayuh*. Everybody's looking to Jake Walther as the likely murderer, but no one is looking at anybody else."

"Seth, you aren't suggesting that Patricia might have murdered her husband."

"I'm not suggesting any such thing. But I am talking sense. The only suspect is Jake Walther. What about Patricia? Wives have killed husbands before. And what about that son of theirs, Robert? Barely showed any emotion about his father gettin' murdered, at least according to what I've heard."

He was right, of course. Not that I suspected Patricia or Robert Brent of being capable of doing such a dreadful thing. But with all the focus on Jake Walther, it seemed that Mort and his deputies hadn't looked beyond him. Yes, there had been speculation—no, make that *hope*—that Rory Brent had been murdered by a passer-through, a stranger, someone with no connection to Cabot Cove. We all fervently wished that.

But what if he had been killed by a Cabot Cove resident—someone who knew him well, someone whom we all knew well? Rory was a popular citizen. He knew many people, maybe the majority of Cabot Cove's population. And because he was a prosperous farmer, he'd undoubtedly had many business dealings, perhaps with someone who became angry at the way a business deal came out.

"You know all the basic reasons for someone murderin' somebody else, Jessica—passion, greed, money, family tensions. Could be somebody got real mad at Rory and flew off the handle."

I shook my head. "I don't think so, Seth, not

the way Rory was killed. It was a deliberate act, well thought out in advance. Maybe not *too* far in advance, but it certainly wasn't a sudden flare-up that resulted in physical harm to him. Somebody wanted to kill Rory Brent—and did."

"I suppose you're right. Did you get a chance to talk with Mort while you were over at headquarters?"

"No. I just stayed long enough to lend some moral support to Mary. Mort wanted them to stay a little longer to answer some questions. I left."

"More tea, Jessica?"

"No thanks. I'd better be running along. I promised myself some time for Christmas shopping."

"What will you be getting me this Christmas?"

I laughed. "I have a very special present in mind for you, Dr. Hazlitt, and wild horses could not pull it out of me. You'll just have to wait until Christmas Eve."

I'd be spending Christmas Eve, after festival activities had ended, with Seth at his home, along with twenty or so other guests.

"Got a special present picked out for you, too," he said.

"Tell me."

"Wild horses couldn't pull it out of me," he said.

I finished my tea and was about to leave when his doorbell rang. I accompanied him to the door. Standing on his wide, wraparound porch was a television crew, led by a middle-aged man. I looked beyond them and saw Mort Metzger getting out of his sheriff's car and heading up the walk.

"And who might you be?" Seth asked the reporter.

"Gary Kraut, Portland TV," the man said. "We just arrived in town to report on the Rory Brent murder. We understand you were his physician."

Seth glared at them.

Mort joined us, and they immediately turned their attention to him.

"You're the sheriff," Kraut said. "What's new in the Brent murder?"

"Excuse me," Mort said and turned to Seth and me. "Got a minute?"

"Of course," Seth said. The three of us returned inside and closed the door in the face of the television crew.

"I just left Joe Truco," Mort said, removing his Stetson and placing it on a small table in the entrance hall.

"You did?" I said, thinking of my request that Turco research public real estate records in Town Hall.

"Thought it only right to run the news past him before acting on it," Mort said.

"What news?" I asked.

"About Jake Walther."

"Stop beatin' around the bush, Mort," Seth said. "Just tell us what the news is."

"Well, seems the lab boys have gotten their act together. No doubt about it, they tell me. The footprint on Rory's barn floor is a perfect match to that boot owned by Jake."

I thought back to what Joe Turco had said, that unless that match was made, Jake would probably remain in the clear.

"Interesting development," said Seth. "What happens now?"

"I've got a call into the D.A.. Hope to meet with her before the day is out," Mort responded. "Seems to me there's nothing else to do but go arrest Jake."

"Again?" Seth and I said in unison.

"Afraid so, Mrs. F.," Mort said.

"Think this time it'll stick?" Seth asked. "Folks in this town are getting downright tired of Jake Walther goin' in and out of jail."

Mort looked at Seth with a hurt expression, as though his good friend was being critical of his police work.

"Didn't mean anything by it, Mort," Seth said. "But you get my drift. Seems to me if you arrest Jake Walther again, it had better be for good this time."

"I wouldn't argue with that," Mort said. "Reason I came by was to ask you, Mrs. F., if Mary Walther, or that strange brother of hers had anything else to say when you were with them."

"No," I said. "The only thing of substance Mary said is what she told you at headquarters."

"Just checkin'," Mort said. "I'll leave you two to whatever it was you were talkin' about."

"I was just leaving when you arrived," I said.

"Got those media vultures outside," Mort said.

"Tell 'em to go away," Seth told our sheriff. "They're on private property up on my porch."

"I'll do just that. Need a lift, Mrs. F.?"

"I think I'll take you up on that, Mort, considering they're outside. Drop me in town where I can do some shopping?"

"Certainly will. Christmas shopping?"

"Yes. I—"

"Got any ideas about what you'll be gettin' me for Christmas?"

Seth and I looked at each other.

"Jessica and I have just been talking about that, Mort. You'll have to wait until Christmas Eve."

"Just remember that if it's clothing, I don't like green. Always had a funny feeling about green clothes, like they were bad luck."

I sighed, smiled, and said, "Mort, I promise the tie I buy you will not be green."

"A tie? I've got a closet full of ties. I was thinking more along the line of—"

"Come on," I said, picking up Mort's Stetson from the table and handing it to him. "If I don't get downtown, I'll never get my shopping done."

Chapter Twenty

I made a silent pledge to myself as I got out of Mort's car in the middle of town that I would blot out everything having to do with murder for the rest of the afternoon.

Although I'm not especially fond of shopping in general, Christmas shopping is another matter. I take great pleasure in finding just the right gift for those I love, and was not about to allow a self-imposed pall to taint that activity.

"I'd appreciate it, Mrs. F., if you wouldn't mention what I told you to anybody else," Mort said, leaning across the seat and speaking to me through the open passenger window.

"Count on it," I said. "You will let me know if Jake is brought in again."

"Yes, I will," he said, resuming his place behind the wheel. I started to walk away, but he stopped me. "If I were you, I'd stay far away from the Walther farm. No telling how Jake will react if he gets wind I'll be taking him in again."

I nodded and said, "Thanks for the advice, Mort. Talk with you later."

Actually, I'd already done some of my Christmas shopping. Seth Hazlitt loves miniature soldiers, particularly those from the Civil and Spanish-American wars. He has elaborate displays of them in his office, and I'd ordered a set from a shop in London whose card I'd taken the last time I was there. They would be arriving by mail any day.

I started at the far end of town, going from store to store, consulting my list of gifts to buy as I went, and thoroughly enjoying the process. The shopkeepers were in excellent spirits, and I found the perfect gifts for a number of people on my list.

Mort Metzger loves board games and had once invented a murder mystery game that he came close to selling to Parker Brothers. But the deal fell through at the last minute over certain changes requested by the company that Mort refused to make. One of our local gift shops had just received a brand-new game, a whodunnit set in Los Angeles. I bought that, as well as a fancy new cribbage board for Mort, making sure that none of the inlaid pieces on the board or the pegs themselves were green.

I would have continued shopping except that my load of gifts had gotten heavy. I decided to call it a day and head for home. I checked my watch. It was almost five. Night had fallen; it had become noticeably colder.

"Call Dimitri for you, Jessica?" the owner of the last shop asked when I mentioned I was going to my house.

"If you wouldn't mind," I said.

Dimitri's cousin, Nick, arrived a few minutes later, helped me load the packages into the back of his vehicle, and drove me home. The timers had turned on my outside lights, one of which cast an appealing glow over the large wreath on my front door.

I thanked Nick, signed the receipt, and got out of the cab.

"I will help you in with the packages," he said.

"Thank you," I said. "I didn't realize I'd bought so much."

"Because you have so many friends," he said pleasantly, loading his arms with the bags and boxes and following me to the front door. I opened it for him. He carried the gifts into my living room and placed them on the couch.

"Thanks, Nick," I said. "That was kind of you."

"No problem, Mrs. Fletcher." He is fond of saying "no problem" in response to most comments made to him by customers.

As I escorted him back to the front door, we were both brought up short by a sound emanating from the rear of my house. It sounded as though someone had tripped over something and fallen.

"What was that?" I said.

Nick didn't answer. Instead, he returned to the living room and approached the door to my study. Another sound was heard, this time a door opening.

Someone was there!

Nick entered the study, with me bringing up the rear. I'd just reached the open doorway when I saw someone swing an object at Nick. It caught him on the side of his head and sent him sprawling to the floor.

"Who are you?" I shouted.

With that, the figure lurched across the room and ran through open French doors leading to a small patio at the back of the house. I didn't see him clearly; it was too dark, too gloomy, for that. None of the lights in the room had been on. But as he ran out to the patio, one of the outside lights caught his face and torso for a fleeting second.

It was Robert Brent!

Or was it?

I fought the urge to take pursuit. Instead, I dropped to my knees next to Nick, who now sat up and massaged the back of his neck and side of his face, groaning as he did.

"Are you all right?" I asked.

"I think so," he said weakly.

"My God, why would such a thing happen," I asked myself aloud as I stood, went to the wall, and flipped on the overhead lights. Nick had been struck with a foot-tall metal cup, the largest of a set of four I'd purchased in Turkey many years ago. Fortunately, the set was not made of heavy metal, and the damage to Nick was minimal. He seemed more shocked than physically injured.

I helped him to his feet. He immediately went to the open French doors and peered out beyond the lighted patio into the darkness. His assailant was gone, presumably having jumped over hedges lining the perimeter of that end of the property.

"Close the doors," I said. "He's gone."

Nick secured the doors, turned, and faced me. "Who would do such a thing?" he said. "In your own house."

"I don't know."

Although I thought the person I'd seen was Robert Brent, I couldn't be certain of it. It had all happened so fast. It looked like him, but if I were asked to attend a police lineup, I knew I would never be able to say beyond a doubt that he was the one who'd been in my house moments ago.

"You must call the police," Nick said.

"Yes, you're right. Please, sit down. Would you like some tea, coffee? A drink? Brandy?"

He shook his head. "No, Mrs. Fletcher, I am quite all right. Please, call the sheriff."

Mort Metzger and a deputy were at my house within minutes. Mort ascertained that the intruder had entered through a window in a small bathroom just off my study. Obviously, using the French doors to escape was a lot quicker and easier than retracing his steps through the window.

"You didn't get a look at him, Mrs. F.?" Mort asked.

"Well, I did, but only for a second. Not long enough to *really* know who it was."

Mort fixed me with a skeptical stare. "Sounds like you're fudging a bit. Sounds like you did see who it was, but don't want to say because you can't be a hundred percent sure."

"It looked to me like . . . I hate to say this, because you're right. I can't be sure. It looked to me like Robert Brent."

"Rory and Patricia's boy?"

"Yes. Again, Mort, it happened so quickly that—"

"Saw his face?"

"Yes. Well, not so much his face. It was his hat and jacket."

"Hat and jacket?"

"He wore a blue baseball cap backward, and a black-and-red wool mackinaw."

"Did he now? Seems to me Robert Brent wore that the day he came into town with us."

"Exactly."

Mort scribbled something on a pad he carried, looked at me, and said, "I think I'll head out to the Brent farm and have a talk with young Mr. Brent."

"I suppose that's what you have to do."

"Have you checked for anything being stolen?" he asked.

"No. I haven't even thought about that. But as you can see, whoever it was was looking for something in my desk." Drawers had been opened, and papers tossed on the floor.

"Well, Mrs. F., I suggest you do a quick inventory, see if anything's missing. You can let me know about that later. Right now, I'd like to hightail it out to the Brent farm. Want Tom to stay with you?" He indicated his deputy.

I shook my head. "No, I'm fine, just fine."

"You okay, young fella?" Mort asked Nick.

"Yes, sir, I am all right. I was glad I was with Mrs. Fletcher and could scare him away."

"Probably was a good thing you weren't alone, Mrs. F. Well, make sure you lock the doors behind me."

They all departed, leaving me alone in the house. I felt an intense chill, which had nothing to do with air temperature. More a reaction to the reality that someone had violated me and my home.

As I walked around the house, looking for signs that something had been taken, I kept hearing noises. I knew they were in my mind, irrational responses to what had just happened, but I couldn't help it.

I settled down and made myself a cup of tea before tackling the task of picking up the papers that had been strewn about my study, and checking to see whether any documents were missing. It seemed to me nothing was gone, although it was hard to make that judgment.

I kept seeing the face I'd seen in the light of the patio. It *was* Robert Brent—or maybe it wasn't. The only thing I was sure of was that the intruder wore a blue baseball cap backward on his head and a black-and-red wool mackinaw. Hardly enough to accuse him of having been the one to break into my home. From what I'd been able to observe, wearing a baseball cap backward had become almost a uniform for teenagers. That the cap was blue wasn't helpful. Most baseball caps are blue, aren't they? A red-and-black mackinaw? Hardly a unique item of clothing in Maine in winter.

If only there had been a second more for me to observe him. The last thing I wanted was to falsely accuse someone.

Seth called a half hour later. He'd heard from Mort about what had happened and wanted to check on me.

"I'm fine," I said. "When did Mort tell you? Had he already gone out to the Brent farm?"

"I don't know, Jessica," Seth replied. "He called

me from his car, said I should ring you up to make sure everything was all right. That's what I'm doin'."

"And I appreciate it, Seth."

"How about some dinner?"

"I don't know. I'm kind of beat from shopping today."

"And all shook up by what just happened to you."

"That, too. I'd love dinner with you."

"Fine. Pick you up in forty-five minutes. We'll go to Simone's. That all right with you? I've had a yearning all afternoon for their special veal chop."

"Fine with me," I said. "I'll be ready when you arrive."

Forty-five minutes later, I had my hat and coat on and was ready for Seth's arrival. But as I stood in the foyer, I remembered I'd left my house keys on my desk in the study. I went there and surveyed the desk. They weren't there. I circled the desk to see whether I'd knocked them off. I had; they were resting on the carpet just enough under the desk to have escaped my initial attention.

When I bent down to pick them up I saw the sheet of paper jutting out from behind my wicker wastebasket. Assuming it was something that had been removed from my desk by the intruder, or was a piece of paper I'd tossed at the basket and missed, I picked it up and was about to wad it into a ball for disposition when I realized it was nothing I'd seen before.

I stood up straight and examined it in the light. It was a note made from cut-out letters from magazines and newspapers, the sort you see in kidnap ransom notes in the movies. The letters were crudely pasted on the paper, forming a jumble of letters, large and small.

But what they spelled out was unmistakable: *Butt out, if you know what's good for you.*

Chapter Twenty-one

Seth and I had just finished a shrimp appetizer and were considering what to have as a main course when Phillipo Simone, the gregarious owner of the restaurant, came to the table.

"You have a telephone call, Mrs. Fletcher," he said.

"Really? Who knew I was coming here?"

"Must be Mort," Seth said. "I left a message for him that we'd be here this evening."

I followed Phillipo to the bar, where he handed me the receiver.

"Hello?"

"Sorry to interrupt your dinner, Mrs. F.," said our sheriff, "but thought you'd want to know that it *was* Robert Brent who broke into your house."

"It was? Are you certain?"

"Certain as I am that Christmas is coming," he said. "The boy admitted it the minute I confronted him."

Mort didn't know about the note I'd found in my study just before leaving for dinner. I'd shoved it into my handbag and taken it with me, and had shown it to Seth shortly after arriving at Simone's.

"Have you arrested him?" I asked.

"Yes, ma'am. He's cooling his heels in cell number three as we speak."

"Mort, there's something else you should know."

"Oh?"

"Whoever broke into my house—Robert Brent, you say—left a note for me."

"A note? What kind of note?"

"The words were spelled out with letters cut from magazines and newspapers. It said, 'Butt out if you know what's good for you.' "

"What does that mean?"

"I don't know."

"Why didn't you give it to me when I was at your house?"

"Because I didn't know it was there. I discovered it on the floor as I was leaving for dinner with Seth. I have it with me."

"I'll be right over," Mort said.

I returned to the table and recounted my conversation for Seth.

He thought in silence, then asked, "What do you make of all this, Jessica?"

I shrugged. "Obviously, Robert Brent left the note in order to intimidate me. But I can't be certain about his motivation. Does he think I've been poking my nose into his father's murder? If so—and even if I was—why would it concern him, unless—"

Seth finished my sentence. "Unless he killed his father and views you as a threat to him by proving it."

Now, it was my turn to be silent. Somehow, the idea that a son would shoot a father in cold blood was anathema to me. Granted, Robert Brent was not your average young person, at least in terms of social skills and outlook on life. Children have killed their parents in the past, and it was naive of me to rule that out based solely upon my refusal to accept the possibility. Still, I wasn't at all convinced that simple tension between a father and son would lead to such a dreadful act.

My thoughts gravitated to Jill Walther and her having sought counseling when she became pregnant in her senior year. Rory Brent, Robert's father, had made that five-thousand-dollar contribution shortly after Jill visited Thomas Skaggs at his agency, Here-to-Help. Jill Walther and Robert Brent had been classmates. When I raised his name during my coffee with her at The Swan, she'd visibly reacted, was angry that I'd even mentioned him.

Was Robert Brent the father of Jill's aborted child?

Had Rory Brent made that large donation to

Here-to-Help in order to cover up his son's involvement in the pregnancy?

The problem with that scenario was that I couldn't conceive of Jill Walther and Robert Brent having had an intimate relationship. They were polar opposites—she the quiet, achieving young woman; he the brooding, marginal student with a sour view of the world.

But I'd learned long ago to never question why any two people get together. Many of my friends over the years have ended up in relationships that didn't make sense to me, or anyone else viewing it from the outside. Yet there was obviously an unnamed, mysterious attraction between them that others were not expected to fathom.

Seth said nothing.

"What are you thinking?" I asked.

"I'm thinking that Robert might have left that note on somebody else's behalf."

"I hadn't thought of that."

Phillipo Simone came to our table and asked what we wished to order as an entree.

"Any specials tonight?" Seth asked.

"Of course," Simone said, grinning. "There is always a special dish for our favorite doctor and writer." He described a veal dish in exquisite detail, and we both ordered it, along with a salad.

"Wine?" Simone asked.

"Not for me, thank you," I said. Seth ordered a glass of Chianti; I opted for a glass of water. I considered a bottle of mineral water, but had decided a long time ago that paying premium prices for water in a bottle didn't make any sense, especially since Cabot Cove's natural water is excellent.

We changed subjects and chatted about things other than the episode at my home that evening. Naturally, the Christmas festival came up, and we discussed in greater detail how we would approach our reading of Christmas stories to the children. We were well into that topic when Mort Metzger entered the restaurant, removed his Stetson, greeted Phillipo Simone, and came to our table, followed by Simone carrying an extra chair.

Once Mort was seated, Seth asked him about the circumstances leading to Robert Brent's confession.

"I drove out to the Brent farm," Mort said. "I beat the kid there by a half hour. I'd no sooner gotten out of my car and was walking up to the house when he comes flying in like a bat out of hell in a pick-up truck. He didn't see me at first, and got out of the truck. When he spotted me, he panicked and jumped back in the truck to make a getaway. I stopped him and asked where he'd been. He had guilt written all over his face, that's for certain. I asked him if he'd been at your house, Mrs. F., and he blurted out that he had. He said he went inside to get warm." Mort laughed, "Some excuse, huh? I told him I was putting him under arrest for breaking and entering, and maybe a few more things. He looked at me with that blank expression of his and said, 'Okay.' "

"Was Patricia Brent there?" I asked.

"I didn't see her. There were lights on in the house, but I figured I didn't have any obligation to go tell her what I was about to do. I put the kid in my car, and we drove back into town. Read him his rights, told him he was entitled to have an attorney present. He just mumbled a few things, so I put him in the cell."

"Will he be charged?" I asked.

"*Ayuh*. I'll take him before Judge Coldwater in the morning. You'll have to be there, Mrs. F."

"Why?"

"To testify. Tell the judge what happened."

"But I'm not the one bringing charges," I said. "You and the district attorney will do that on behalf of the state."

"We could, but it would have a lot more clout if you showed up."

I looked at Seth, who nodded.

"All right," I said.

"Now, what about this note?" Mort asked.

Before I could respond, Mr. Simone came to the table and asked the sheriff if he wished anything.

Mort looked at Seth's glass of wine and said, "Can't drink 'cause I'm still on duty. Maybe just one of your antipasto platters and a glass of that nonalcoholic beer."

Seth, who'd been looking at the note earlier in the evening, handed it over. Mort's brow furrowed as he digested it.

"What do you make of it, Mort?" Seth asked.

"Doesn't seem to be any debate about what it says, or means," our sheriff replied. "Looks like young Mr. Brent was trying to scare you off."

"We understand that, Mort," I said, "but the bigger question is scare me off from *what*?"

"Has to do with Rory's murder. Seems pretty simple to me," Mort said.

I was tempted to tell him about Jill Walther's pregnancy and the possible link to Robert Brent, but knew I couldn't do that without breaching Seth's confidence. Mort carefully folded the note and put it in the pocket of his blue down winter uniform jacket. "Wish you hadn't touched this," he said. "Could be prints on it."

"I never stopped to think. I was running out the door, spotted it on the floor, grabbed it, and brought it with me," I said defensively.

"No harm, I suppose," Mort said.

Phillipo's son, Vincenzo, who worked with his father at the family restaurant, delivered Mort's antipasto platter and bottle of Buckler beer.

"More than I can eat," Mort said. "Help yourselves."

Seth and I glanced at each other and smiled.

We'd never seen a platter of any size that was more than Mort's voracious appetite could handle.

Mort stayed throughout the dinner, and we left the restaurant together. To our surprise, it had started to snow, lightly and gently.

"Weatherman didn't say anything about snow," Seth grumbled, raising the collar of his overcoat and pulling it tight around his neck.

"You folks take care, drive easy," Mort said, tipping his hat.

"Same to you," Seth said.

As Seth drove me home, I asked absently, "I wonder why it took Robert Brent the length of time it did to drive home after leaving my house."

"Probably stopped off for a Big Mac," Seth said.

"Possibly. Or, maybe he stopped to see someone."

"Like who?"

"I don't know." I turned and faced him. "Jill Walther?"

"I don't think so," was Seth's response. "Can't imagine him going to the Walther farm, considering everything that's gone on."

"Maybe he met her some other place. Maybe they had a date."

"Always a possibility, I suppose," Seth said, turning into my driveway, which now had a thin coating of fresh snow on it.

"Cup of tea?" I asked.

"Thank you, no. Sure you'll be all right alone here tonight?"

"Of course I will. Robert Brent was the one who broke into my house, and Robert Brent is sitting in a jail cell. Nothing to worry about."

"I suppose you're right. Well, Jessica, sleep tight, call me in the morning."

"I will. And thanks for dinner. It was excellent, just what I needed."

As was his custom, Seth walked me to the door and waited until I'd opened it. Before I did, however, I saw that a large manila envelope was propped against it. I picked it up. My first name was written on it in big letters.

We stepped into the foyer, and I opened the envelope. A handwritten note was attached to a sheaf of papers.

Jessica—Here's what I came up with at Town Hall re: the Walther property. Hope it's helpful. Pay particular attention to the info on Rory Brent's "other life." He had more money than anyone knew. I checked on the partnership he was involved with in Indianapolis. An eye-opener. Happy reading. Sorry I missed you. Will call in the morning. Joe.

"What's that all about?" Seth asked.

I explained that I'd asked Joe Turco to see what

he could find at the town clerk's office about the Walther farm.

"Why did you do that?"

"Curious, that's all. Jake Walther and Rory Brent allegedly argued about land and money. I just thought public records might provide a hint as to what might have prompted that argument."

"I see. Well, looks like you've got some reading to do. Frankly, I can never make sense out of legal papers. All full of gobbledygook and boilerplate legalese."

I laughed. "I'll do my best," I said. "Thanks again for dinner. Careful home. The roads are slippery."

Despite my bravado about being alone in the house that night, I found myself apprehensive once there. I kept thinking of earlier that evening: the sound of someone intruding upon my sacred place, seeing the person run out the French doors, and believing it was Robert Brent; the papers from my desk strewn all over the floor. I'd been fortunate. Evidently, the only reason Robert came to my house was to look for something in my desk, and to leave his sophomoric note warning me to "butt out." Inflicting serious bodily harm wasn't on his agenda.

Still, there was something unsettling about being where an intruder had stood only hours earlier.

I tried to put it out of my mind, turned on the

television set, and settled back to watch the news, the papers Joe Turco had delivered resting unread on my lap. I surfed the channels, using the remote control, until landing upon the Fox News network, where Roberta Brannason was filing a live report on the Rory Brent case from the steps of City Hall.

"I'm Roberta Brannason reporting from Cabot Cove, Maine, where one of this charming town's most beloved citizens, Rory Brent, a prosperous farmer and a man who brought joy to the village each year as Santa Claus at the annual Christmas festival, was murdered in cold blood. We've been reporting to you on the progress of this case, which has shaken Cabot Cove to its foundation. Now, Fox News has learned that an arrest is imminent. The prime suspect all along has been another farmer, Jake Walther, a man universally disliked by most citizens of this Maine community. He's been detained, then released on two occasions. Now, reliable sources have told us that the laboratory analysis of a footprint found on the dirt floor of Rory Brent's barn does, in fact, match the sole of one of Mr. Walther's boots . . . and that the sheriff of Cabot Cove, Morton Metzger, in concert with the local district attorney, will once again arrest Mr. Walther and charge him with the murder of Santa Claus. I'm Roberta Brannason reporting from Cabot Cove, Maine."

I clicked off the TV, sat back in my recliner, closed my eyes and sighed.

I thought of Mary Walther, and, of course, her daughter, Jill. What a tragedy to have a member of your family accused of having murdered another person. The pain must be unbearable.

I placed the papers on a table next to my chair, got up, went to the window, and peered through the glass. It was still snowing, although it hadn't intensified. I returned to my chair and waited for the TV weather report. Our local weatherwoman—local in the sense that she reported from a station in Portland; Cabot Cove does not have its own TV outlet—said that we shouldn't expect much in the way of accumulation, and that the snow would stop before dawn.

Although dinner had been delicious, it sat heavy on my stomach; too much food without enough time to properly digest it. I considered taking a walk, but the weather dissuaded me. Instead, I went to the cabinet in which I keep liquor and poured myself a small snifter of half brandy and half port wine.

Years ago, when coming back to the Scottish mainland from the Orkney Islands, we'd hit vile weather, so bad that I wondered halfway through the trip whether we'd make it. Obviously, we did, but I stepped ashore a shaken person, and with an extremely upset stomach. I went into a hotel near the dock and asked the bartender for a small glass of blackberry brandy, which I'd always considered good "medicine" for an upset stomach. The bartender, an older Scottish gentleman, suggested I instead try a mixture of port and brandy. "Make you feel like a new person," he told me.

His advice proved right. My stomach immediately settled down, and I enjoyed a big dinner before heading for my hotel in another village along the coast.

I took a sip of my medicinal concoction and focused my attention on the events of earlier that evening. It was obvious that Robert Brent had left the note to scare me. What I couldn't figure out was what he might have been looking for in my desk. What sort of paper would be of interest to him, so much so that he would break into my home and risk arrest?

My pondering of that question was interrupted by the ringing phone. I glanced at a clock on the wall; it was eleven-thirty, late for someone to be calling, especially in Cabot Cove, where most people lived the adage of early to bed, early to rise, including me.

"Hello?"

"Mrs. Fletcher?"

I recognized Jill Walther's voice.

"Jill?"

"Yes. Did I wake you?"

"No, although I was about to head for bed. I watched the news and the weather."

"Mrs. Fletcher, I have to talk to you."

"I'm happy to hear that, Jill. I wanted very much to see you again before you returned to school. Your mother said you'd be cutting short your vacation."

"Yes. That was her idea."

Her tone was accusatory. She didn't sound at all happy that her mother had made the decision for her to prematurely leave Cabot Cove.

"Why don't we get together tomorrow? Breakfast? My treat."

There was a long, profound silence on the other end of the line.

"Jill?"

"Yes. I'm sorry. Could you come to the farm?"

"Tomorrow?"

"No, right now. I wouldn't ask except . . . Mrs. Fletcher, I'm so scared."

"About what?"

"About everything. About my father and what might happen to him. About me. I don't think I could go back to school knowing my father is accused of Mr. Brent's murder. I couldn't face anyone. I saw the news tonight, too. They keep talking about my father having killed 'Santa Claus.' That isn't fair. I can't stand having people think of me as the daughter of someone who murdered such a popular person as Mr. Brent."

"I think you might be overreacting, Jill. Most people don't blame a family member for the act of another. Besides, your father hasn't been proved guilty of anything."

She began to sob, softly at first, then more urgently.

"Please, Jill, get hold of yourself. I don't see how I could come to your farm tonight. I don't drive and—"

"I'm sorry, Mrs. Fletcher. I never should have made this call. This isn't your concern."

"Oh, but it is, Jill. I took a very special interest in you, and that interest continues to this day. I want what's right for you, no matter what your father might have done. And I stress the word *might*. Maybe I can get someone to drive me out there—the local cab company."

Her toned brightened. "Would you?" she said. "Thank God. You're such a wonderful person and—"

"I'll call and see if they'll pick me up. It might be too late for them, although at this time of year they tend to work later. People getting ready for Christmas, that sort of thing. If you don't hear from me, I'll be there within the hour."

"Thank you again, Mrs. Fletcher. I knew I could count on you."

Dimitri answered on the first ring.

"Are you still working?" I asked.

"Yes, ma'am. My cousin worked all day, and I'm driving at night. A busy time of year."

"Yes, it is. Dimitri, could you pick me up at the house and take me out to the Walther farm?"

"Now?"

"Yes."

"Of course I can, Mrs. Fletcher, but—"

"But what?"

"Why do you want to go out there at this time of night, and in this weather?"

"Oh, the weather doesn't seem to be a problem. It isn't much of a snowfall. I have to go out there to . . . well, to deliver some Christmas things."

"I see."

I knew what he was thinking, that it was an odd time of night to be delivering Christmas gifts. But I didn't elaborate, nor did he ask me to. He simply said he would be at my house in fifteen minutes.

I used the few minutes I had to peruse the public land records Joe Turco had dropped off. As Seth said, they were loaded with legal boilerplate, and I had trouble digesting what they said. But it wasn't a completely futile exercise. I was in the process of going back to reread a section concerning ownership of the Walter farm when Dimitri arrived. I shoved the papers in my bag, left the house, and joined him in his taxi.

Although it was a light snow, it did create slippery road conditions, and Dimitri drove slowly and carefully. As we approached the Walther farm, he asked which of the three houses he should take me to.

"The middle one," I said.

He turned onto the rutted dirt driveway that led into the farm and stopped at the house shared by Mary and Jill Walther. It hadn't occurred to me to ask Jill whether her mother was there. I assumed she would be. When I thought about that, I wondered why it was Jill who'd made the call, and not Mary. Had Mary encouraged her to do it? Did Mary share in her daughter's fear?

I had a choice of asking Dimitri to wait for me, or to dismiss him and call him later. "I will wait for you," Dimitri said.

I was about to tell him not to bother, but the thought of having him outside was comforting.

"I appreciate that," I said. "Just charge me for whatever time you have to wait."

"That is not a concern, Mrs. Fletcher. I will do whatever is best for you."

I slid forward on the backseat and placed my hand on his shoulder. "Thank you," I said. "You're a good man."

I had noticed as we came up the road that there was a light on in the first cabin, the one occupied by Jake Walther, and that smoke drifted from the chimney. Lights were also on in the middle cabin. I looked beyond it to where Dennis lived. That cabin was dark.

I got out and shivered at the sudden change in

temperature between the warmth of Dimitri's car and the cold outside air.

I went up the steps, stepped onto the porch, and knocked. Mary Walther opened the door.

"Good evening, Mary," I said. "I know this is late to be visiting but—"

Her tone was as stern as her face. "I know why you're here, Mrs. Fletcher. Because of my silly daughter."

"Silly? She called and asked me to come because she was frightened. That's why I'm here."

Mary Walther's large body filled the open doorway. She pressed her lips tightly together, narrowed her eyes, and said, "As long as you're here, you might as well come in."

She stepped back, allowing me to enter the living room, and closed the door behind us. It was toasty warm in the house, and the smell of freshly baked cookies wafted from the kitchen.

"A nasty night, although they say the snow will stop by morning," I said, making conversation.

"She shouldn't have called you," Mary said.

"Jill? I don't know whether she should have or not, but I didn't see any alternative but to respond. She sounded upset. Is she here?"

"Upstairs."

"May I see her? Will you go tell her I'm here?"

"She doesn't have to!"

We both turned at the sound of Jill's voice, who stood on the narrow staircase leading to the second floor, arms folded across her chest, defiance painted on her face.

Mary said sweetly, "Why don't you get some cookies and tea for Mrs. Fletcher, Jill."

"No need for that," I said.

"As long as you're here, we might as well be good hostesses." Her voice firmer now. "Get cookies and tea for Mrs. Fletcher."

I watched as Jill made up her mind what to do. Then she slowly descended the stairs and disappeared into the kitchen.

"You're right," Mary said. "She's very upset. I suppose she's entitled to be, but that's why I insisted she leave here and go back to school. There's nothing but negative feelings because of what Jake did."

"Because of what Jake did? Are you saying he murdered Rory Brent?"

"I can't defend him any longer, Mrs. Fletcher. Lord knows, I want to. He's my husband, and I don't want to see him go to jail. What will we do here without him? We'll lose the farm. But it seems certain now that Jake did kill Rory. I can't say that I blame him. Rory Brent, with all his so-called niceness, was not as nice as people thought."

"I'm sorry to hear that from you, Mary. May I take off my coat?"

"If you're intending to stay."

"I don't mean to intrude, and I'm not here to

see you. I promised Jill I'd come and talk to her. I intend to do that."

"Suit yourself, although you won't get much sense out of her. She's just a wreck, schoolgirl sort of emotions. Crying all the time, wailing about what her life is going to be like because of what Jake did. I told her to get a grip on herself. Lord knows I've shed my tears, but I've done it in private. What we have to do now is face reality. My husband murdered another man, and they have the proof of that. He'll have to face the consequences, and so will we, but we'll do it with dignity."

I admired her staunch stand. She undoubtedly had had to exhibit this sort of inner strength throughout her adult life as Jake Walther's wife. Not only was he an unpleasant man, his efforts at farming had not resulted in much financial gain. Many woman I know would have bolted, run from such a situation. But Mary had stayed, and obviously intended to stand tall no matter what fate befell her and her daughter.

Jill reappeared carrying a plate with Christmas cookies in one hand, and a mug of steaming tea in the other. I took off my coat, placed it on a chair, and sat at a small table. Jill placed the plate and mug in front of me.

"The cookies look good," I said, thinking it must be especially hard to do anything in the Christmas spirit under the circumstances.

"Life must go on," Mary said. "Mrs. Fletcher, I—"

"Please, Mary, call me Jessica. I'm here as a friend."

"You keep reminding me to call you by your first name, but I find it difficult. You're a woman of substance and of the world. Famous and rich. I was brought up to be respectful of my superiors."

"I am not superior to anyone or anything."

I turned to Jill. "Want to sit down and tell me why you asked me to come here tonight? I'm sure whatever is causing you such concern can be worked out, and I promise I'll help any way I can."

Jill looked to her mother as though to gain permission to speak.

"Go ahead, Jill, tell her whatever it is you want," said her mother. "Get if off your chest. Maybe once you do you'll stop acting so silly."

Jill and I looked at each other.

I said, "I'm waiting, Jill."

She averted her eyes and took a few breaths as though pumping herself up for what she was about to say. Finally, she said flatly, in a statement that sounded as though she'd rehearsed it, "My father did not kill Mr. Brent."

I looked at Mary, who said, "See? Denial. Just denial all the time." She said to Jill, "You have to stop this, Jill. You have to grow up and face facts. Neither of us wants to admit that Daddy killed Rory Brent. I've been denying it to myself ever since it happened, and there's a side of me that keeps saying he didn't do it. But he did, Jill, and that's the cruel truth."

I asked Jill, "Why do you say your father didn't do it? I mean, I understand that you want it that way, but do you have a solid reason, some evidence that would prove his innocence?"

She looked straight at me and said, "Ask Dennis."

Mary guffawed. "Here you go again. Dennis told the truth when he said he was not with Daddy the morning of the murder. Dennis was with me. We were attending to the chickens and trying to fix that damn wall that keeps falling down on the coop."

"That's not true," Jill blurted, standing straight and clenching her fists, as though about to do physical combat. "Dennis would say anything that you tell him to, and you know it."

Mary extended her arms at me and said, "See? I get no help from her. She's calling me and Dennis liars. Some daughter. She's out of her mind. The best thing for her is to be away from here and back at school."

What Jill had said a few moments ago about Dennis doing whatever Mary told him to do interested me. Until then, it had been assumed that any possible influences on Dennis's story had come from either Jake—who allegedly threatened him with physical harm if he didn't tell Sheriff

Metzger that they'd been together the morning of the murder—or from the sheriff himself, suggesting to Dennis that he might want to change his story. It wasn't that Mort would have done anything like that deliberately. But if Dennis was as suggestible and malleable as people said, it was possible that Mort had inadvertently led him into a different version of events.

Was Jill right? Had Mary exerted control over Dennis, helping him shape his recounting of events that morning to suit herself? Why would she do that? What would she have to gain from seeing to it that Dennis testified in a certain way?

I asked Mary, "Do you have any doubt in your mind that Dennis is reporting what actually happened that morning, Mary?"

A dark, severe expression crossed her broad face. "Are you suggesting, too, that I'm lying?"

I laughed to soften the moment. "Of course not. But Dennis has a reputation for being easily influenced. That's all I meant."

"People think a lot of bad things about Dennis because he's slow. But I assure you, Jessica . . . Mrs. Fletcher . . . that he's not a liar. He's a good and decent man who works hard and keeps to himself. That's the way we were brought up as brother and sister."

Not wanting to further anger her, I turned my attention to Jill, who'd regained her seat on the bottom step of the staircase. I wasn't sure what the reaction would be if I raised the question of her visit to Here-to-Help to obtain counseling, including the option of abortion. I certainly would have preferred to ask her about that in a private setting, just between the two of us. But I had the sinking feeling that the only opportunity I was going to have to speak to her was here and now, in this small, modest home in which she'd grown up, and in the presence of her mother who, I now realized, was more domineering than I imagined.

I decided to broach the subject obliquely.

"Jill, when you and I had coffee the day of Mr. Brent's funeral, I mentioned his son, Robert. You said you knew him because you were classmates."

I searched her face for a visible reaction and found it. It was a combination of surprise, fear, and anger.

"So?" she said.

"Do you know that Robert broke into my home earlier this evening?"

Her stutter-step response said clearly to me that she was aware of it.

"No. I mean . . . broke in? . . . No . . . why would I . . . ?"

I continued. "Robert has been arrested and is in jail now. He left me a note, Jill, warning me to, as he put it, 'butt out.' "

Nervous glances were exchanged between mother and daughter.

"Have you seen him tonight?"

"Seen who?"

"Robert Brent."

"No. I mean, why would I see him?"

Mary, who'd been sitting in a narrow ladder-back chair, now stood, placed her hands on her sizable hips, and glared at me from her elevated position. "Maybe it's time you left," she said.

I sighed, shrugged, and said, "I will leave, of course, if you want me to. But I have a feeling, Mary, there's something more going on here having to do with Rory Brent's murder than you're willing to admit."

I didn't give her a chance to respond. I looked at Jill. "Jill, I know about what happened in your senior year. I know you went to seek counseling in Salem with the Here-to-Help organization. Mr. Skaggs? Remember him?"

I braced for a response. It came from Mary Walther.

"You obviously have been doing a lot of snooping into this family's business," she said.

"I prefer not to call it snooping, Mary. I have become involved in the investigation of Rory's murder due to circumstances that I didn't create. But now that I am, I think I owe it to myself—no, let me amend that—I think I owe it to this town to help get to the bottom of what happened so that it can be put to rest, hopefully before the Christmas festival and everything good and decent it represents."

Jill started to say something, but caught the words before they came out.

"You have no right doing this," Mary said.

"I'm not doing anything, Mary, except trying to get some answers. Which, I might add, could help your husband. I don't believe he murdered Rory Brent."

"You don't?" Mary said. "What makes you such an expert in murder? You write books, that's all. The evidence is against him, as sad as that might be. Please leave."

I stood and went to where Jill continued to sit. I placed my hands on her shoulders, brought my face close to her, and said softly, "Sometimes, Jill, keeping painful secrets weighs too heavy on us. What happened in high school was a mistake, a tragic one, of course, but a mistake. You don't have to live the rest of your life suffering for it."

I straightened and turned. Mary held out my coat for me to slip into. I did, retrieved my hat and scarf from where I'd dropped them on a table, and went to the door.

"I wish you didn't view me this way," I said. "Believe it or not, Mary, all I want to do is help you and your family."

"I think the best way to help my family is to leave us alone," she said.

"Fair enough."

As I reached for the doorknob, I was startled by the sound of heavy footsteps on the porch outside. My hand froze in mid-motion. There was no need for me to open the door because Jake Walther did. He pushed it open with such force that it almost knocked me over. He stepped inside and slammed the door behind him.

He had a crazed look in his eyes.

The smell of alcohol on his breath was overwhelming.

And the sight of the shotgun he carried was sobering.

Chapter Twenty-two

To say Jake's sudden arrival shocked me would be an understatement of classic proportions. Although he didn't physically touch me, his mere presence caused me to back up as though I'd been pushed.

"Cozy little group you've got here, Mary," he said, his words slurred.

"Go back to your house," Mary said with authority.

Jake glared at me. "You just can't keep your nose out of our business, can you?"

"I came to visit your daughter," I said, forcing calm into my voice. "I was just leaving."

"Maybe you ought to stay a spell," he said. There was a distinct threat in his voice.

"No," I said. "I have someone waiting for me outside."

He grinned and said, "He won't be missing you."

"What do you mean? It's Dimitri. He drove me here. He's waiting for me to—"

"Dimitri ain't waiting for nobody," Jake said. "I took care of that."

"You haven't hurt him, have you?" I said.

"Just made sure he wouldn't be worryin' about when you come out."

"Excuse me," I said, moving toward the door. "I'll see for myself."

He shifted position so that my path was blocked. "What's everybody been tellin' you tonight, Mrs. Fletcher?"

Realizing I was not about to be allowed to leave, I returned to the table. "What I've been told," I said, "was that Mary has become resigned to the fact that you'll be arrested for Rory Brent's murder."

"Yup. I heard that on the radio. Matched up my boot, did they, with the footprint on ol' Rory's barn floor?"

I looked directly into Jake's watery, bloodshot blue eyes and said, "I don't believe you killed Rory Brent."

My words seemed to stun him into a moment of sobriety.

I continued. "I came here only to talk to Jill. I took a deep interest in Jill and her future when she was in high school, and that interest hasn't waned."

I turned to Jill. "Jill, I know what happened to you in your senior year of high school."

Mary erupted. "I'll have none of that talk in this house."

I said to her, "I know it's none of my business, Mary, at least not personally. But I can't help feel that what happened to Jill in high school has a bearing upon Brent's murder. Do you know that shortly after Jill visited Here-to-Help, the social agency in Salem, Rory Brent made a large contribution to that organization?"

No one replied.

"Why did he do that?" I asked. "We all know that Rory was a prosperous and generous man, but what did Jill's pregnancy have to do with *him*?"

My mention of the word *pregnancy* hit the room with all the impact of an exploding grenade. Mary was barely able to contain her rage. Jake, whose rigidity had lessened, sagged against the door.

"Jill," I said, "please tell me why Mr. Brent would have done that. It's not because I'm prying into your life. I have no right to do that. But if it helps identify who killed Rory Brent, it's important that you be honest with me."

Jill said softly, "He did it because of—"

"Shut up!" Mary Walther shouted, turning, and approaching her daughter.

"Why not tell her?" Jill said, standing. Although she was considerably smaller than her mother, she now matched her in defiance. "It's all going to come out anyway, no matter how hard you try to keep it quiet."

Mary turned to her husband. "Tell her to stop it, Jake." Again to Jill, "Go upstairs to your room."

"No," Jill said.

"It was because of Robert Brent, wasn't it?" I said.

When she didn't respond, I went to her, placed my arm around her shoulders, and said, "Jill, honey, it's all right. This kind of thing just keeps festering inside us unless we face it head-on. Was Robert Brent the father of your child?"

My back was to Mary and Jake. I heard shuffling behind me, but thought nothing of it. My attention was too intently focused upon Jill, who had started to weep silently. She pressed against me, and I wrapped my arms around her. She said in a voice so soft I could barely hear, "Yes."

"Jill, did Mr. Brent arrange your abortion?"

The noise behind me had stopped. Jill dabbed at her eyes with the back of her hands and slowly shook her head.

"Who did then?"

"No one. I . . . I had the baby."

A muttered curse from Mary Walther caused me to turn. Mary had taken the shotgun from Jake. It was pointed at me.

I was surprised at how calmly I said, "Put the shotgun down, Mary. This can all be worked out.

The important thing is that the pieces be put together so that Rory Brent's murder is solved, and we can get on with our lives. All of us. Christmas is almost here. What's happened to you and your family is tragic, and I ache for you. But don't do anything to make it worse."

"You just don't understand, do you?" Mary said. "You've lived a charmed life, never had to worry about where your next meal was coming from, never had to wonder what people were saying behind your back. I know how people view Jake and me in this town. Do you think I'm stupid?"

"Of course not."

"You write your books and travel all over the world, live in a nice house, have money in the bank. Like most folks in Cabot Cove. But we've struggled just to survive ever since we bought this farm and tried to make a go of it. It's never been easy. But we always kept our dignity, always believed in ourselves as a family. And we had a daughter. There she stands, Ms. Jill Walther. All our hopes were with her, that she'd make something of herself and the Walther name. But then she went and got herself pregnant with that bum, Robert Brent, and everything we hoped for went up in smoke."

I said to Jill, "You said you had the baby. While you were in school?"

"Yes."

"I never even knew you were pregnant," I said.

"Nobody did," Mary said. "She never showed much. Couldn't even tell she was carrying. Had the child down in Salem at some home for girls like her. Was there just a few days. Called in sick to school."

"Where is the child now?" I asked.

"Adopted," Mary said. "Don't know who. They don't tell you such things."

"You poor girl," I said to Jill. "Have you seen your son since giving birth?"

"It was a girl, Mrs. Fletcher. A little girl. I named her Samantha."

"Samantha," I repeated absently. "Did Rory Brent make that donation to keep your pregnancy quiet and to protect his son?"

Mary answered for her. "Mr. Big Shot, Rory Brent, wanted Jill to end the pregnancy. He sent her to that agency, hoping they'd talk some sense into her."

"I take it Mr. Skaggs at Here-to-Help did just the opposite," I said, feeling a sudden warmth for the bearlike man who ran Here-to-Help.

"He urged me to have the baby," Jill said. "And I did."

"Was Mr. Brent angry with your decision?" I asked.

"Sure as hell was," Jake Walther said. "Said he'd bury us all if we didn't do things the way he wanted."

I smiled at Jill. "But you stuck to your guns."

"Yes, ma'am."

"But if sending you to the agency didn't result in ending your pregnancy, the way Rory wanted it to end, why did he make that large contribution?"

"Because I told him I intended to have an abortion," Jill said."

"You lied to him?"

"I didn't know what to do, what was right and what was wrong. I decided to keep my baby. He sent the money before I changed my mind."

Brent having sent five thousand dollars to Tom Skaggs at Here-to-Help was an act of supreme arrogance. He'd wanted Skaggs to convince Jill to end her pregnancy, and was rewarding him for it. Good for you, I thought, looking at Jill.

Discovering that my thesis had been wrong— that Jill had had an abortion—forced me to shift gears and to try to fit this new piece into the scenario under which I'd been operating. What took front and center in my thinking at that moment was the role this information possibly played in Rory Brent's murder.

I asked Jill, "What did Rory do after he learned that you decided to keep the baby?"

Her mother answered for her. "Oh, Rory Brent was hopping mad." She looked at her husband. "Wasn't he, Jake?"

"Yup," Jake muttered.

"Mr. Rory Brent liked to call the shots," Mary continued. "He didn't want his precious son to have to take financial responsibility, and said he'd see to it that he never had to."

"What did he mean?" I asked.

"He said that if Jill didn't give up the baby, he'd trash her so bad—trash us—we might as well be dead. We weren't in no position to argue with him. If Jill kept the baby, that would have ended her dreams, and ours, too. Another mouth to feed? We've had trouble putting food on the table just for us."

"Did you want to keep the baby, Jill?" I asked.
"Yes."

"But your parents urged you to give it up because of finances?"

Jill didn't answer. I looked to Mary and Jake, but they, too, said nothing.

Jill had again sat on the bottom step of the staircase. I sat next to her and took her hand in mine. I then said to no one in particular, to the room itself, "Why was Rory Brent killed?"

Jake and Mary Walther looked at each other. It was Jake who spoke. "The man was no good, Mrs. Fletcher. Him and that goddamn son 'a his. Raped Jill and—"

"That's not true," Jill quickly said. "Robert and I . . . we got together, that's all, sort of found each other. The other kids never liked me much, or him. A couple of nerds. It just happened, that's all. One day at his house."

"Jake," I said, "if someone was mad at Robert

Brent for getting Jill pregnant, why would he kill his father?"

"For trying to use what his son did to our daughter to blackmail us, hold it over our heads," Mary said. "Jake just snapped, that's all. Had enough from that so-called saint, Rory Brent. *Mr. Santa Claus.*"

I stood and said, "You didn't kill him because of what happened between Jill and Robert."

"What are you saying?" Mary said.

I pulled the envelope from my purse that had been left at my house by Joe Turco, opened it, and removed the papers it contained. "Rory had taken your farm from you."

Mary reached for the papers, but I kept them from her reach. "You were about to lose the farm to the bank. Rory lent you the money to save it, but charged exorbitant interest and attached an impossible repayment schedule. If you didn't meet the deadline to pay it back, the farm was his. And that's exactly what happened, isn't it?"

Mary started to say something, but I cut her off.

"You weren't the only ones to have this happen," I said. "I'm not certain how it worked, but these papers indicate Rory was involved with a company in Indianapolis, a partnership of some kind that made its money identifying farmers who'd fallen on hard times, lending them money with their farms as collateral, and taking the farms when they couldn't make the payment. They've been doing it all over the country for years. It's called loan sharking in big cities."

I waited for an answer.

"You got it right," Jake said.

"So now, you know what happened," Mary said. "Can you blame Jake for wanting him dead?"

"No," I said. "I don't blame Jake at all—because Jake didn't murder Rory Brent."

Mary glared at me.

"You killed him, Mary."

Mary's response was flat, void of emotion. She slowly lowered the shotgun and said, "That's all we had left, the farm. It never gave us much, but at least we had a roof over our heads and a place to grow vegetables." Her voice gained strength. "Everybody walked around talking about what a wonderful person Rory Brent was. He wasn't wonderful, Mrs. Fletcher. Sure, on the outside he looked like a perfect gentleman, putting on his Santa Claus costume every year, giving to charity, everybody loving good old Rory. But he was an evil man. He wouldn't have cared if he put all of us in the ground. He and Jake had an argument about a month before about him taking the farm from us. I wanted Jake to do something, but what could he do? Look at him." She turned and extended her hand to her husband. "Jake's just a dirt-poor, hardworking man who drinks too much and lets the world stomp all over him. But he's always tried, for me and for her." She pointed at

Jill. "But sometimes you can't let people walk on you, Mrs. Fletcher. Sometimes you have to take matters into your own hands and right a wrong."

"And you shot him to right that wrong," I said.

"Don't say nothin' more, Mary," Jake said.

"It doesn't much matter," Mary said. "I couldn't believe I did it. I went to talk sense to him, ask him to be fair and to let us stay till we found the money to pay him back. When I arrived that morning, I saw him leave the house and walk to the back barn. I followed him inside and pleaded with him, put my heart in my hand and offered it to him. All he did was laugh, Mrs. Fletcher. Oh, excuse me. Jessica. I forgot I'm supposed to call you by your first name, real friendly like. Rory said me and Jake were losers and didn't deserve to have this piece of property. He called Jill a slut, said she seduced Robert and wasn't any better than her mother and father. He just kept saying things like that until I couldn't take it anymore. So yes, I shot him, shot him dead, and walked away not feeling guilty one bit."

I walked to where Mary stood and took the shotgun from her hand, then placed it on the table. "Mary, I'll help in any way I can. No matter what happens, it's important that Jill go on with her life, continue her education, and become the fine writer I know she will."

I turned to Jake, "You knew Mary shot him, didn't you?"

" 'Course I did. I figured they'd think it was me 'cause of my reputation. We had Dennis change his story so that Mary would have an alibi. I was hoping that if nobody could prove it was me, they wouldn't ever think of her. You kind of knew all along, didn't you?"

I shook my head. "No, I didn't, although I started to suspect when I learned that your boot had once again been matched up by the laboratory to the footprint in the barn."

I said to Mary, "I remember once being in a shoe store with you. You had to buy a man's moccasin because none of the women's sizes fit you. It occurred to me that you might easily have worn Jake's boots that morning and left the footprint in the barn. Did you do that deliberately, to make Jake the suspect?"

"No," Mary said. "It just happened that way. I always wear Jake's boots when I'm out and around."

"What about Dennis? Why did he lie?"

"Like I said, to protect her," Jake answered. "Dennis and me were fixing a fence that morning, just like he first said. But after she shot Rory, we wanted folks to think it was me."

"And you were willing to go to jail, maybe even the electric chair, to save her."

"Like she said, Mrs. Fletcher, we may be dirt poor, but we know we're family. All we've got is each other."

This time, when I went to the door, no one attempted to stop me. I opened it and looked outside.

"What did you do with Dimitri?" I asked.

"Nothin'," Jake said. "Just told him to get out of here, to get off my property before I blew his brains out."

As he said it, I saw lights approaching, some of them flashing. A moment later, Sheriff Mort Metzger pulled up the road and stopped outside of the house. Dimitri was in the car with him, along with two deputies.

"You okay, Mrs. F.?" Mort asked as he ran up onto the porch.

"Yes, Mort, I'm fine."

"Dimitri came and got me. Told me he'd dropped you here, but that Jake ran him off the property with a shotgun. I figured I'd better get out here pronto."

"And I appreciate that, Mort. But everything is fine now. I think if you talk to Mary, you'll be able to put the Rory Brent murder in your file of solved cases. In the meantime, I am very tired and would appreciate a lift home."

Chapter Twenty-three

" 'Who said that?' "

"The kindly old man looked around. Someone had said 'I'm hungry.' But as far as he knew, he was the only person in the house that Christmas morning."

Seth and I continued to read from "The Dog That Talked at Christmas," the story of a lonely old man who'd found a stray puppy in a snowstorm on Christmas Eve. In front of us this Christmas Eve were more than a hundred small children, their eyes bright, their attention totally focused on this charming tale of all creatures, great and small, sharing in the Christmas spirit.

" 'Could I please have something to eat?' The old man spun around and looked down at the puppy. 'Did you say that?' he asked, his eyes open wide," Seth read.

I followed with, "The puppy said, 'All I said was I'm hungry.' "

Behind us on a large screen, color illustrations from the book were projected to coincide with the story's progression. Seth and I alternated paragraphs.

" 'You can talk? But you're a dog. Dogs don't talk.' "

" 'Oh yes we can,' the puppy said. 'We're not supposed to, but I'm so hungry.' "

"The old man sat and stared at the puppy. A talking dog, he thought. A Christmas miracle. He could become rich with a talking dog, go on television, make commercials, become famous."

" 'All dogs can talk,' said the puppy. 'But we know that if we do, we'll have to go to work. Don't tell any other dogs I broke the rule. They'll be very mad at me.' "

"The old man made them a hearty breakfast, and the puppy gave him a big, wet kiss. Tears came to the old man's eyes. He'd been alone for so long. Having this Christmas puppy filled his house with joy and love. 'Your secret is safe with me,' he told the puppy. 'But you will talk to *me*, won't you?' "

" 'Of course I will.' "

The final picture came to life on the screen— the puppy and the old man together beneath the Christmas tree.

" 'Good night,' the old man said."

" 'Good night,' said the puppy."

"Merry Christmas!" we said in concert.

The kids got to their feet and applauded. Cynthia Curtis came from the wings and congratulated us on a wonderful performance.

"Suppose I'd better get back to the house," Seth told me. "Still some preparations to go for the party."

"Yes, you have twenty guests coming."

"And you have another performance."

"I know." I raised my eyebrows and sighed. "I can't believe I agreed to do it. I'd better get dressed."

His grin was wicked. "Can't think of a better person to play Santa, Jessica. But don't let the little tykes cough in your face. Bad flu season coming up."

A half hour later, after having pillows strapped to my waist and being outfitted with a brand-new Santa costume purchased by the festival committee, I sat in a large chair, propped a steady stream of children on my lap, and heard their wishes for Christmas presents. Roberta Brannason's TV crew and the one from Portland filmed the action.

When the last child had told me what he wanted Santa to bring—some sort of expensive video game I'd never heard of—Ms. Brannason approached.

"You make a great Santa," she said.

"Thanks. But I think I'll retire from the job. Not easy."

"You made it look easy, Mrs. Fletcher, like you

were born to it. Now that the Brent murder has been solved, how about an interview?"

"About the case? Nothing to say."

"No, not about the murder. About being the first female Santa Claus in Cabot Cove festival history."

I couldn't help but laugh. I'd removed my false white beard and red hat, enjoying the cool air on my face and head. I said, "Give me a minute to get this beard back on, and I'll be happy to speak with you on camera."

The interview went well, and was actually fun. It gave me the opportunity to extoll the festival, the village, and the wonderful people who made Cabot Cove a special place at Christmas.

"Thanks a lot, Mrs. Fletcher," Brannason said. "I really appreciate it."

The TV folks left, and I was about to go backstage to shed my Santa uniform when the door opened at the rear of the school gym. Jake Walther and his daughter, Jill, stepped into the gym and looked around. Jake had on his bib overalls, but wore an ill-fitting suit jacket over it. Jill was dressed in a pretty red-and-green dress suitable for the season. They slowly approached.

Hello," I said. I was about to add "Merry Christmas," but thought better of it, considering Mary Walther had been arrested and was in prison this Christmas Eve.

"Merry Christmas," Jill said.

"Merry Christmas," I said. "Hello, Jake."

"Mrs. Fletcher," he said.

"You look great in that costume," Jill said.

"And I can't wait to get rid of it. I'm surprised to see you."

"Didn't want to come," Jake muttered, "but the girl dragged me here."

I smiled. "I'm glad she did."

"Mrs. Fletcher," Jill said, "I just wanted to come and thank you for everything you've done."

"My goodness," I said, "I'm afraid there are no thanks in order. After all, I am responsible, to a great extent, for your mom being where she is at the moment."

"You did what you had to do," Jake said.

"I'm glad you see it that way, Jake."

"Mr. Turco says he'll do everything he can to help Mary," Jake said. "She's a good woman. Never been in trouble her entire life. I guess the pressure got a smidge too much for her."

I didn't respond.

Jill stepped close to me. "The reason I wanted to come here was to ask Santa for something for Christmas."

"Oh?"

"I wanted to ask Santa that he—I guess Santa is a *she* this year—that she pay a little extra attention to a little girl in Salem, Maine, named Samantha. At least I assume she's still there."

I fought to hold back the tears.

"I just know she's with a wonderful family who's giving her a special Christmas. But I thought that maybe Santa would put in an extra good word for her."

"You can count on it, Jill," I said. "And I'm sure you're right. Samantha is having a wonderful Christmas with a family that loves her very much."

"Thanks, Mrs. Fletcher."

It occurred to me that there was a wonderful, meaningful story in what had transpired with Jill Walther, a story she could write from the heart. As fiction, of course. Maybe I'd suggest it to her at another time.

"Well," I said, "time for me to get back into my civilian clothes. I'm going to a party at Dr. Hazlitt's house."

"Don't want to hold you up," Jake said. "Much obliged for how you've helped Jill with college and all."

"It's been my pleasure, Jake. Where are you going now?"

"Back home, I reckon," he said.

I was certain they didn't have a Christmas tree, or any other vestiges of the holiday season. I wondered if they even had any festive food.

"Would the two of you like to come to Dr. Hazlitt's Christmas Eve party?" I asked.

Father and daughter looked at each other.

"Please," I said. "As my special guests."

"I don't figure I'd be welcome there," said Jake.

"Don't worry about that," I said. "I'll see to it that you're made to feel very much at home. After all, this is Christmas."

An hour later, my Santa uniform having been shed, and dressed in my holiday finery, I went with Jake and Jill Walther to Seth's house, where the Christmas Eve party had begun. When we first walked through the door, the expression on people's faces was of surprise, even shock. But Seth broke the tension by coming to Jake and Jill, extending his hand, and saying, "Welcome, Jake. Hello, Jill. Merry Christmas. Help yourselves. There's plenty 'a food for everyone."

The party broke up at eleven, and most guests headed for their homes to spend the remainder of Christmas Eve around their own trees with family. Mort Metzger, his wife, Jim and Susan Shevlin, and Seth and I handled the clean-up chores. Once the house had been put back into some semblance of order, we sat in the living room.

"It was a nice thing you did, Mrs. F., bringing Jake Walther and his daughter here," Mort said.

"They seemed to enjoy themselves," I said. "No matter what Mary did, they shouldn't have to pay for it. How is she holding up in jail, Mort?"

"Pretty well. Prays a lot. Gives us no trouble. She'll be off to the county lockup in a few days. Better facilities there. Jake and Jill visited her this afternoon. Brought a Christmas wreath and some cookies to cheer her up. I feel bad for Jake. He really wanted to be in that cell instead of his wife. Was willing to take the rap for her, and would have, if you hadn't intervened, Mrs. F."

"The festival was a success," our mayor, Jim Shevlin, said. "Best ever."

"You always say that, Jimmy," said Seth.

"But it was the best," Susan Shevlin said, "thanks to you, Jessica."

I waved her compliment off and said, "Actually, being Santa Claus wasn't as bad as I thought it would be. I kind of enjoyed it."

"I wasn't talking about playing Santa," Susan said. "What saved the festival was having Rory Brent's murder solved before the festival. Having it hanging over the town as an unsolved crime would have put quite a damper on things."

"What do you think will happen to Robert Brent?" Seth asked our sheriff.

"About breaking into Mrs. F.'s house? Up to her if she wants to press charges." They looked at me.

"I don't intend to press any charges," I said. "Actually, it was somewhat touching the reason he broke in and left that note. He'd gotten wind that I knew about Jill's pregnancy and wanted to help her keep the secret. As he told you, Mort, he was looking for any papers I might have had concerning it. In some ways he's nicer than his father was."

"I still have trouble knowing that Rory wasn't as nice a guy as everybody thought," Seth said. "Sort 'a challenges your faith in mankind."

"I don't feel that way," I said. "Yes, it is disillusioning that he was part of a group that preys on people like the Walthers. Hundreds of others like them all over the country. But it hasn't destroyed my faith—in anything. Peace on earth, goodwill toward men."

"And women," Susan said.

"All living things," Mort's wife said.

"Yes, all living things," I repeated.

"Deck the halls with boughs of holly, fa la la la la, la la, la la."

We went to the window and looked out at the dozen men, women, and children making the rounds singing Christmas carols. They waved; we returned the greeting. A few flakes of snow could be seen in the flickering flames of the candles they carried.

Eventually, the others left, leaving me alone with Seth. Vaughan and Olga Buckley had planned to be there, but canceled at the last minute. I wasn't disappointed, although I always love to see them. But it was nice having some quiet time for myself, shared at that moment with my good friend, Seth.

At a few minutes before midnight, he handed

me a small glass of sherry, raised his glass to touch rims with me, and said, "Merry Christmas, Jessica."

"Yes, Seth, Merry Christmas."

To all.

Here's a preview

of the next

Murder, She Wrote

Mystery

Murder at the Powderhorn Ranch

When I announced to my friends in Cabot Cove that I intended to spend a week at a Colorado dude ranch, their response was one of incredulity.

"You don't know how to ride a horse, Mrs. F.," Sheriff Mort Metzger said. "Might fall off and hurt yourself."

Another friend, Dr. Seth Hazlitt, said, "You write murder mysteries, Jessica, not cowboy books. Better off spendin' a week at a place you can use in your next novel."

They meant well, but their reactions didn't dissuade me. I'd already accepted an invitation from old friends, Jim and Bonnie Cook, who'd left Maine years ago to fulfill their dream of owning and operating a guest ranch in Colorado. They'd called me last week. "It's time you came out here for a visit," Jim said. "Bonnie and I have a horse all picked out for you, the trout are jumping, and one of our best cabins has your name on it. Besides, we're always looking for another square dance partner."

"Please come," Bonnie added. "It's been years. We miss you."

I decided on the spot to accept. I'd just finished a book and didn't intend to start the next for a few months. A relaxing week at their ranch, The Powderhorn, in Powderhorn, Colorado, forty-five minutes outside of the town of Gunnison, was exactly the break I needed.

Three weeks later, on a lovely late August day, I boarded a flight from Boston to Denver and connected with a flight to Gunnison. Jim Cook met me at the airport. Soon, I was sipping tea with my good friends in their spacious log home.

Now, with a solid night's sleep, and a hearty breakfast in the lodge under my belt—and some basic riding instruction from one of the ranch's four young wranglers—I mounted my horse for the week, a splendid chestnut trail horse named Rebel, and joined a string of other guests on horseback for our first trail ride into the spectacular, rugged hills and mountains surrounding the ranch.

Accompanying us were Jim and Bonnie's two dogs—Socks, a border collie who earned his keep by herding the ranch's horses at feeding time, and Holly, a mixed breed with a sweet disposition and a penchant for crashing through bushes and brush in search of small animals.

It had been a chilly forty degrees when I got up. Now, with the sun rising high into the deep blue sky, it had warmed up to sixty, a typical pristine day on tap in Western Colorado.

Initially, when we left the corral, I was tentative being so high off the ground. I hadn't been on a horse in years, and Rebel was a big one, the largest of the ranch's forty-two steeds. But after an hour, I settled into a comfortable synergy with his gait and felt as though I'd been riding him all my life. Adding to the pleasure of having become one with my horse was the sheer joy of being there: the views became increasingly breathtaking as we continued our ascent, the horses were surefooted on the narrow, twisting rutted trails winding through groves of aspen trees and ponderosa pines. A hawk circled overhead; chipmunks scurried across the trail; and deer watched impassively from a safe distance.

The other guests that week were from one family, the Morrisons, and a couple who'd arrived at the last minute, Paul and Geraldine Molloy. Jim and Bonnie had explained that each year the Morrison clan gathered for a family reunion at the Powderhorn, the annual event arranged by Craig Morrison, the oldest of four brothers and a wealthy real estate developer from Denver. Nine Morrisons attended this year's reunion, including

Craig. But only six were on the ride this morning. Craig was working in his cabin, according to another brother, Chris, whose wife, Marisa, joined us on horseback that morning. Craig's teenage son and daughter were also part of the riding group, as was an unmarried cousin, Willy, and the family matriarch, Evelyn Morrison, a patrician woman who looked younger than her years, and whose youthful figure nicely filled out the jeans, designer plaid shirt, and down vest she wore. She rode tall and erect in the saddle, her hair perfectly coifed beneath a black Stetson studded with rhinestones. An impressive group, I thought upon meeting them at breakfast, proud of what was obviously a staunch and successful family. Mrs. Molloy rounded out our group.

We stopped on the ridge of the mountain we'd climbed to stretch our legs and take in the vistas. Our wrangler, a young woman named Amber, pointed out various mountain peaks in the far distance, and identified some of the wildflowers that painted the countryside with bursts of color.

"Ready to head back?" Amber asked.

"Whenever you are," Chris Morrison said.

The teenagers had wandered off, and we had to round them up before mounting our horses and starting back down the series of trails that had led us to the top.

"Enjoying yourself, Mrs. Fletcher?" Evelyn Morrison asked as we slowly retraced our steps.

"Immensely so," I said. "This is paradise."

"Will you be setting one of your mysteries on a guest ranch?"

"Goodness, no. This is vacation time for me. No books, no plots, no nefarious characters, and certainly no murders. *Especially* no murders, at least for a week."

She laughed.

"Can't we go faster?" one of the teens asked. "This is boring."

"We go as fast as our guide allows us to go," the family matriarch said haughtily.

"Grandma looks like a cowboy," his sister said, laughing.

"*Cowgirl* is more appropriate," Evelyn said. "And I have told you countless times not to call me Grandma. I am not old enough to be your grandmother. I am Evelyn."

I kept my smile to myself. Evelyn Morrison was obviously as vain as she was beautiful.

It was a little past noon when we turned onto the final trail leading to the ranch. We rode in single file; I'd ended up first in line directly behind Amber. Evelyn was directly behind me, followed by the rest of her family.

It was when we reached flat ground and were on a dirt road, the ranch looming in the distance, that Holly tore off into the bushes and barked.

Amber brought us to a halt and said, laughing, "That's the first time I've ever heard her bark."

The dog continued to sound off, barking at one moment, whining the next. Socks, her canine step-sibling, joined her.

Amber signaled us to resume the ride, and slowly headed down the road. I started to follow, but as I passed where the dogs were making a ruckus, I saw something out of the corner of my eye. I pulled on the reins, bringing Rebel to a halt. The others halted behind me.

"What is it?" Evelyn Morrison asked.

I pointed to the bushes.

"What?" she repeated.

"That," I said, referring to the lower portion of a human leg that had been uncovered by the dogs' thrashing about.

"It's a leg," Chris Morrison said.

"Ugh," the teenage girl said.

Amber got down off her horse, handed the reins to me, and went to where the dogs waited, tails wagging. She parted the bushes with her boot and leaned over to see better.

"What is it?" Evelyn Morrison said in a voice she undoubtedly used when demanding answers from underlings in boardrooms.

"It's—"

Amber stepped back as though physically pushed, and returned to us.

"It's—it's Mr. Molloy," she said.

"Molloy?" Evelyn said.

"My husband?" Geraldine Molloy said.

"Yes," said Amber.

"Oh, boy," Cousin Willy said.

Evelyn turned to face her son, Chris. "Get back to the ranch and call Walter in Denver. The phone is in the laundry room."

"Walter?" I said.

"Our attorney," Evelyn replied.

"It must have been an accident," Cousin Willy said.

I climbed down from Rebel, handed the reins to Amber and stepped closer to the body. Amber was right. It was Paul Molloy. After observing his bloody face, I straightened up, turned and said, "This was no accident. This was murder."

"So much for your idyllic vacation, Mrs. Fletcher," Evelyn Morrison said. To the others: "Stop gawking and follow me. We have things to do."

PENGUIN PUTNAM

online

Your Internet gateway to a virtual environment with hundreds of entertaining and enlightening books from Penguin Putnam Inc.

While you're there, get the latest buzz on the best authors and books around—

Tom Clancy, Patricia Cornwell, W.E.B. Griffin, Nora Roberts, William Gibson, Robin Cook, Brian Jacques, Catherine Coulter, Stephen King, Jacquelyn Mitchard, and many more!

Penguin Putnam Online is located at
http://www.penguinputnam.com

PENGUIN PUTNAM NEWS

Every month you'll get an inside look at our upcoming books and new features on our site. This is an ongoing effort to provide you with the most interesting and up-to-date information about our books and authors.

Subscribe to Penguin Putnam News at
http://www.penguinputnam.com/ClubPPI